We'll Always Have Murder

A Movie Memorabilia Mystery

Gayle Leeson

Grace Abraham Publishing
Bristol, Virginia

Dedicated to Tim, Lianna, Nicholas, and to "Detective" T. W. Tilson

Chapter One

My eyes widened as I read the email for the second time. My friend, Barry, who was a set designer in New York, had acquired a copy of a *Casablanca* script with the original title, *Everybody Comes to Rick's*. After scrutinizing the photo Barry had attached to the email, I wrote back asking if he was sure it was an early *Casablanca* script rather than a copy of the play written by Murray Burnett and Joan Alison.

I sent my response and went back to studying the photograph. Whether it was an original movie script or simply a copy of the play upon which *Casablanca* was based, I wanted it. If it was the original movie script, then I would be getting it for a steal. If it was the play, I'd try to haggle with Barry to get it a little cheaper.

Casablanca merchandise sold well at my shop—Lights, Camera, Action!—and this script would be a wonderful conversation piece.

My phone buzzed, and I hoped it was a notification that Barry had replied to my email already. But it wasn't an email from Barry; it was a text from Mom.

Where are you?

I checked the time. Yikes. It was later than I'd thought.

On my way, I responded.

Closing the laptop, I took one last look around the shop. Everything was neat and tidy. Cassiopeia—"Cassie," my part-time assistant—had done a nice job cleaning up before leaving to run home and eat dinner with her dad before going to the theater. Which is what I needed to do too. Not have dinner with Cassie's dad, of course, but I needed to eat and get to the theater.

Had you told me six months ago that I'd be running a successful movie memorabilia shop in Skillet Ridge, Virginia, I'd have said you were crazy. But here I was with the brick-and-mortar store and an online shop, and I felt it was going well. I wasn't making a fortune by any stretch of the imagination; but I was making ends meet, doing something I loved, and rebuilding relationships with my mother and my sister.

Waving a hand in the direction of the *Conan, the Barbarian* corner, I said goodnight to the mannequin that bore a passing resemblance to Mr. Schwarzenegger. I tapped the button to engage the electronic lock and left.

As I drove toward my mom's house, I realized I wasn't the only one whose life had undergone a drastic change these past few months. I'd come back home to work as a set designer for a movie called *Claiming Victory*, which had been filmed here in my hometown. The movie had put Skillet Ridge on the map in much the same way *The Hunger Games* had done for Shelby, North Carolina.

My plans to return to New York had changed after my sister's car accident. Patty hadn't been hurt as badly as she could have been, but she'd really messed up her left arm. And her life was in shambles. She'd wrecked her car while fleeing their home in tears after finding her husband in a compromising position with a coworker.

Now Patty was a widow. Her husband was murdered—but that story would take too long to explain here. Suffice it to say, Patty didn't kill him and is recovering from a lot of physical and emotional trauma.

From the corner of my eye, I glimpsed something on the side of the road. I checked to make sure there was nothing behind me before slowing the car to a crawl.

It was a white cat. And it was merely sitting there. It would be lucky to survive if it got out into the road.

Putting on my hazard lights, I pulled over to the side of the road a few feet in front of the cat. I wished I had something to feed it to make it come to me, but I didn't. It probably didn't matter. The poor thing was probably scared and would run.

I got out of the car and started walking toward the cat. "Hey, kitty. Come on. Let's get you out of this road before you get hurt."

It watched me, making no attempt to run but not moving toward me either.

"Come on, baby." I looked around at the overgrown fields. Not a house in sight. "Out chasing mice, huh? I have some tuna at home. I bet that would be better than a mouse."

The cat uttered a low meow.

"I know. It's okay." I crouched down and nearly toppled over when a pickup truck blew past me. "See? It's dangerous out here."

As the kitty slowly moved toward me, I remained still, resisting the urge to stretch out my hand. "It's all right."

Coming closer, it sniffed my hand.

"You're a good kitty, aren't you?"

Purring, it butted its head against my hand and allowed me to pet it. After a minute or two, I did something I was afraid I was going to regret. I picked it up.

Rather than scratch or bite, the cat purred even more and nuzzled my neck.

"Good kitty." I carried it back to the car. "I'm sorry I don't have a crate or anything. If you'll bear with me, I'll have you to Mom's house in just a few minutes."

I wasn't laboring under the delusion that the cat understood me, but I hoped it realized I was friendly and was trying to help. And, so, as I sat the poor thing on the passenger seat and it yowled protests, I continued to talk.

Turning off the hazard lights, putting on my signal, and then pulling back out onto the road, I said, "Mom is going to be surprised to see you. I'm already late because I get lost in my work easily. Mom often makes dinner for my sister and me, and I'm usually at the shop most days well past closing. There's always so much to do."

I had to raise my voice over the cat's wailing. "Not much on car rides, huh? Well, we'll be where we're going soon. What do I have to do at work? Is that what you're asking me?"

The cat flattened its ears and looked disgusted that I was foolish enough to believe it had asked me anything other than why I'd put it into a vehicle. But I'd already explained that, I thought, and I figured I'd tell it about the shop.

"Well, I have to keep an eye on movie merchandise and restock when we get low. Customers are particularly fond of *Star Wars*, *The Wizard of Oz*, *The Chronicles of Narnia,* and—of course—*Claiming Victory*. I'm always seeking new and novel items to sell so patrons don't feel like the shop is getting stale. Let's see…. What else keeps me busy?"

I glanced to my right to make sure the cat wasn't about to spring on me. It didn't appear to be. I continued my soliloquy.

"I often change which movies I'm showcasing based on the season or which movies are currently playing in theaters. You know, if there's a horror movie out, I'll showcase *Nosferatu*, *Dracula*, or *The Lost Boys*."

Other than a soft meow now and then, the cat had gone quiet.

"Some of my customers have suggested I get a popcorn machine and sell the buttery snack for them to eat while perusing the shop. I always smile and say it's a good idea, but it's actually a horrible idea. I can't stand the thought of all those greasy fingerprints on my merchandise. I do burn popcorn-scented candles sometimes to add a touch of cinematic ambiance."

I pulled into my mom's driveway. "Here we are." I put the car into park and shut off the engine. And then I sat there waiting for the cat to feel comfortable again. "May I rub your chin?" I reached out tentatively. When the cat didn't draw back, I caressed its chin with my index finger.

The purring didn't start up right away, but it let me continue to pet it. After a moment, it got up, stepped across the console, and settled into my lap. I stroked its soft fur until the purring began. Then I picked it up, got out of the car, and walked into my mother's house where the cat and I were greeted with the delicious aroma of beef stew. My stomach growled, reminding me that I hadn't eaten since breakfast and startling the cat, who gently raised a paw to tap my cheek.

"What's that?" Mom asked.

"It's a cat."

"Why is it in my kitchen?"

"I picked it up. It was on the side of the road, and I was afraid it would get hit by a car." I pulled a chair away from the table and sat down, lightly holding the cat on my lap. "I'll make some flyers to see if we can find its owner. There weren't any houses around where I found it."

She sighed. "All right. I'm not taking care of it, though. Don't even think about asking me to." She went to the pantry, took out a pouch of tuna, and put it on a saucer.

The cat perked up and began meowing.

"Here." Mom placed the saucer on the floor. "But don't get used to this. We'll—I mean, *Dina*—will get a few cans of cat food to tide you over until we find out who you belong to."

I set the cat onto the floor, and it ran to the tuna, eating like it was starving.

"Where's Patty?" I asked.

"She ate her stew and went on over to the theater."

"I'm sorry. It wasn't my intention to be late." I explained about Barry and the script he'd found.

"I always liked the movie *Casablanca*." In one of the worst Humphrey Bogart impressions I'd ever heard, she said, "'We'll always have Paris. Here's lookin' at you, kid.'"

I applauded. "That was something else. You should talk with Patty about getting you a part in *Barefoot in the Park*."

My sister was the manager of the Skillet Ridge Theater Company, and she'd brought me on as the set designer.

"Ha, ha," Mom said. "I know sarcasm when I hear it. Besides, the play is already fully cast."

"Still, you might have fun acting in a play. Maybe you could get a part in the next production."

"We'll see." She took a jug of milk from the fridge. "I'm having this. What would you like to drink?"

The cat looked up from its half-eaten plate of tuna.

"You're getting water," she told it.

"Milk is fine with me," I said, getting two glasses from the cabinet.

"You know, I'm glad your sister has something to throw her energy into, especially after the car accident and all that unpleasantness with Gregory." She poured milk into the glasses and then filled a small bowl with water for the cat.

Unpleasantness. The man had cheated on Patty, caused her to leave the house an emotional wreck and have an accident, and been found dead in my shop. On top of that, Patty and I had been the police department's prime suspects in his murder. Not that Mom was wrong— the ordeal *had* been unpleasant—but she was a master of making light of a horrible situation, that was for sure.

My phone buzzed. I took it out of my pocket and looked down at the screen. I'd received an email from Barry. I opened the email and read, "The script is the real deal, Dina. I have the proper authentication. Want it?"

"Absolutely," I said.

Chapter Two

I slid my chair back from the table, rinsed out my bowl and glass, and put them in the dishwasher. "Thank you for dinner, Mom. That was great. I'm going to go by the pet shop on my way to the theater to get the cat what it will need while we look for its owner. In the meantime, I hope it doesn't destroy my apartment."

"Since your apartment is actually *my* apartment, I feel you should leave the cat here with me. And I can put the cat in the laundry room while I go to the pet store and get a few things for it, in particular, a litter box."

I tried to give her some money for the supplies, but she wouldn't take it.

"Go on," she said. "Your sister is waiting for you."

Giving her a quick kiss on the cheek, I thanked her again and hurried out the door. I felt guilty for saddling her with a cat I'd picked up off the side of the road—I mean, what if it had some sort of disease or something—but she *had* offered. And the cat looked healthy and as if it had been well cared for. Mom had made an excellent point about the litter box. Plus, the poor thing would probably have been frightened had I left it in my apartment by itself all evening. I'd take the cat off Mom's hands as soon as I got back.

When I arrived at the theatre, the scene was mildly chaotic. Cassie's father, Gerald, was there while Cassie and Billy rehearsed a scene on stage.

"Hi, Gerald," I said. "What brings you by?"

"I'm...um...here to make sure the staircase looks okay."

Gerald had helped with set construction and had indeed made the staircase which had been designed to appear as if it wrapped around the right side of the stage.

"It looks great," I told him.

The gruff man merely nodded, his eyes remaining on the stage, giving away the true reason he was there. It was apparent that he wasn't terribly happy that his daughter, who played Corie, the new bride, had so many kissing scenes with Billy, who played her husband, Paul.

Given Gerald's obvious feelings on the matter, I kept my opinion to myself, but Cassie and Billy were both good kids and an adorable couple—perfect for their roles.

As soon as Patty saw me, she rushed over to ask if the phone had arrived yet. I had ordered a beige princess rotary phone from an online auction site as a prop for the play.

"It's supposed to arrive tomorrow," I said.

"I hope it does. The play premieres in just over a week." Patty nervously wrung her hands.

"It'll be here. I'm still amazed I had to order one. Not only do I find it a little strange that there wasn't a rotary phone in the prop room, but I'm also surprised mom didn't have one in the garage or the attic."

"There wasn't one in the prop room because we don't do that many plays that take place in the late 1960s or early '70s—or so I've been told," Patty said.

Neil Simon's *Barefoot in the Park* was Patty's first production as the manager of the theater, and she understandably wanted everything to be perfect.

"Everything is going to be great," I said. "The set looks fantastic, the actors are terrific, and everybody in Skillet Ridge is going to be blown away by this play. You'll be the talk of the town."

"I'll be the talk of the town if it bombs too."

That was true, but I refrained from agreeing with Patty as she hurried off to speak with Cassie and Billy. I was there for moral support tonight more than anything, so I went down and took a seat in the front row to watch the rehearsal.

Patty moved to the center of the stage. "Okay! Let's start from the beginning and run through the entire play."

Billy turned, spotted me in the front row, and gave me a wave before he went backstage. He brought Cassie a furry white coat and put it around her shoulders. She laughed as she huddled into the coat, pretending she was cold.

Since he wasn't in the first scene, Billy came and sat beside me. "How are you, Dina?"

"I'm fine. You and Cassie are doing a wonderful job. I can hardly wait until opening night."

"Yeah," he said, "we're having a really good time. I believe this play is gonna be a success." His eyes darted over to where Gerald still stood just offstage.

"Don't sweat it. He makes me nervous too," I whispered.

He chuckled. "Gerald makes everybody nervous, and I think he likes it that way."

As Billy and I had been talking, the curtain had been lowered. Now it rose on Cassie entering from stage right. She was carrying a bouquet of daisies and looking around for something to put them in. Spotting an empty paint can, she hurried over and picked it up, took it to the sink, and pretended to fill it with water.

While Cassie was arranging the daisies in the paint can, Billy whispered to me, "Isn't she amazing?"

I nodded, wondering if this was anything more than a play romance. During my time working at Brown's Theater in New York, I'd seen many couples fall in and out of love during the course of a production. I hoped neither Billy nor Cassie would end up with a broken heart.

A doorbell buzzed.

Cassie put the paint can full of flowers on a small table, went to the right side of the stage, and shouted, "Hello!"

Phil Lemon, who played telephone repairman Harry Pepper, sounded as if he were in the bottom of the barrel when he called, "Bratter?"

The two carried out the rest of the scene with excellent comedic timing.

Throughout the remainder of play rehearsal, I noticed some odd behavior between Phil, the telephone repairman, the actress playing Corie's mother, and the actor playing the eccentric neighbor, Victor Velasco. On the drive home, I called Patty and asked her about it.

"What's the deal with the phone repairman, the mom, and the neighbor?" I asked.

"In the play, or in real life?"

"In real life. I'm familiar with the play, but I found the dynamic between those three actors really weird."

"Yeah, it is weird. Imelda, who plays Mrs. Banks, and Alfred, who plays Victor, were very lovey-dovey until about a week ago," Patty said. "Phil, who plays the telephone repairman, had been flirting with Imelda since day one, but she had always pretty much ignored him. And then one evening, Imelda and Alfred came in, and it was apparent there was some tension or anger between them. I figured they'd had a tiff like any other couple, but that's when Imelda began responding to Phil's attention."

"Do you think she was angry at Alfred and flirting with Phil to make him jealous? I mean, despite Imelda's flirting with Phil, she still left with Alfred. Are they married or—"

"I have no idea what the nature of their relationship is, and I haven't asked. Their actions are more like those of teenagers than seniors; but as long as they perform their parts well and don't let their personal lives interfere with the production, I feel it's none of my business."

"You've got a point, sis. Live and let live... unless one of them kills one of the others and ruins the play." I laughed.

Patty did not.

Patty and I arrived at Mom's house at approximately the same time. We found Mom on the sofa with the cat curled up on her lap. Mom was watching a movie—a rom-com—and the cat looked up as if it was annoyed that we had disturbed them.

"What's that?" Patty pointed at the cat.

I opened my mouth to speak, but Mom beat me to it.

"Patty, meet Popcorn. Popcorn, this is Patty, my other daughter."

"You got a cat between the time that I left for rehearsal and now?" Patty asked.

"Not exactly," Mom said. "Dina saw it on the side of the road about to get run over."

"There was no near miss or anything," I said, "but I didn't want to take any chances."

"So Popcorn is here with us until we can find his or her owner." Mom stroked the cat's head. "Now, if you two don't mind, we'd like to see the end of our movie."

Patty sighed and said she was going to go on and get ready for bed, and I sat down beside Mom to watch the end of the movie with her and Popcorn.

"When are you gonna have a meet-cute with somebody?" Mom asked me when the movie ended.

"I don't know, Mom. If it happens, it happens. If not, I'm pretty content with my life."

"I'm content, but I'm always on the lookout for a good meet-cute."

That comment mildly alarmed me, so I scooped Popcorn off her lap and said, "Thank you for taking care of the cat this evening. Did you happen to leave a note up on the bulletin board at the pet shop asking if anyone had lost a white cat?"

"You know, I didn't even think about that."

"That's all right. I'll go by the print shop in the morning before work and get some flyers made," I said.

"Oh, don't worry about that. I can go to the print shop. You've had a long day—you'll want to sleep in as long as you can tomorrow morning."

"Thanks, Mom. I appreciate that."

"No problem. You know how I hate to see anything lost and wandering around on its own." She walked over to me and rubbed the cat under the chin. "Don't forget Popcorn's things."

When I saw how much she had bought for the cat, I realized maybe Mom needed a full-time companion. "Would you rather I leave Popcorn here tonight?"

"Well, that would save you from having to drag a bunch of things back and forth."

"Back and forth?" I asked.

"You weren't gonna make the poor thing stay home alone tomorrow, were you?"

Yeah, we were definitely going to have to get Mom a cat.

"I wouldn't dream of it," I said.

Patty wandered into the living room with her phone in her hand. She wore a blank expression.

"What's the matter with you?" I asked. "You look like a zombie."

"I feel like one. I...I...." She shook her head. "This can't be happening."

"What is it?" Mom asked.

"It's Imelda—she's dead."

Chapter Three

I tried to process what my sister had just said—
Imelda is dead. "Did she and Alfred have an
accident on their drive home?"

Patty shook her head. "No. Billy called me. He
works part-time for the lifesaving crew. Imelda was hit on
the head with a blunt object and was found lying in her
front yard."

"That's terrible!" Mom exclaimed. "Do the police
think she was mugged?"

"I don't know," Patty said woodenly. "I don't have
any of the details."

"I'm so sorry." I placed Popcorn on the couch so I
could step over to Patty and give her a hug. "Is there
anything I can do?"

"I don't know," she repeated, staring blankly straight ahead. "I don't know."

"Go get in your bed," Mom told her. "I'll bring you some hot cocoa."

With a slight nod, Patty mechanically left the room.

"Will she be all right?" I whispered to Mom.

"Sure. She's shocked at the news of Imelda's death; and I imagine she's also feeling guilty because she's worried about how the death of one of her actresses will affect the play."

"True." I sighed. "I'm going on home. Call me if either of you need anything." I petted Popcorn on the head. "Do you still want me to leave the cat here tonight?"

"Yes. It'll be a welcome distraction."

As soon as I got up to the apartment, I gave Billy a call.

"Hi, Dina."

"Hey, Billy. What happened to Imelda?"

"All I know is that one of her neighbors was out walking her dog and saw Imelda lying in her yard. She said she called out, but when Imelda didn't answer, she hurried back inside and called 9-1-1."

"Did she see anyone else?" I asked.

"No, but earlier she'd heard a car speed off. The police officers on the scene believe it was Imelda's attacker—or attackers—who fled the scene."

"Where was Alfred?"

"He was at his house when I called him," Billy said. "He was awfully upset."

"I thought maybe the two of them were married."

"No. Just dating, I guess. They're both widowed."

"Was Imelda robbed?"

"The police were still investigating when the other EMTs and I left. But it didn't look to me like it was a robbery." He paused. "Heck, I'd have thought she'd taken a fall and hit her head accidentally, had it not been for the bloody crowbar lying near her body."

I shuddered. "Oh, my."

"Don't worry," Billy said quickly, "I didn't mention that part to Patty. She went all to pieces when I told her Imelda was dead."

"Thanks for sparing her the gory details." I rather wished he'd done the same for me.

"Did…um…did she say anything about the play? Not that our little production is a priority at a time like this. But, you know, I just wondered."

"She didn't, Billy. It seemed to me she was in shock. I imagine she'll call everyone in a day or so."

The next morning, I went to Mom's house to check on her, Patty, and the cat. All three seemed to be all right. Patty was in a much better state of mind than she'd been when I left last night. We discussed what had happened to Imelda over coffee and peanut butter toast at Mom's kitchen table.

"I spoke with Billy last night," I said. "He didn't seem to know much more than what he told you—only that Imelda was murdered."

Patty paused, her coffee cup halfway to her lips. "Imelda was murdered?"

He said he hadn't given Patty the gory details, but I'd assumed he'd told her that someone had taken Imelda's life. I thought that was part of the reason Patty had been so shaken.

As gently as I could, I said. "Imelda was hit over the head with a blunt object."

"Who'd do such a thing?" Mom asked, gathering Popcorn onto her lap, as if the cat might save her from a similar fate.

"Billy didn't know." I took a bite of my warm, delicious toast.

"But surely, the police have a suspect," Patty said.

"All Billy knew when I spoke with him was that the police were investigating." I started to include the bit about his not believing it was a robbery but stopped myself. Billy's speculations weren't going to help Patty and Mom deal with the fact that Imelda was beaten to death in her front yard. I, too, hoped the police had someone in custody, but I wasn't holding my breath. "Patty, I wouldn't be surprised if the police stop by to speak with you, the other theater staff, and the actors."

"Why would they do that?" Mom kissed Popcorn on the head before placing the cat onto the floor, getting up, and retrieving the coffee pot.

Many people had switched to those pod machines, but Mom still preferred her tried-and-true coffeemaker. I was glad—I could always count on Mom having a fresh pot of coffee in the mornings.

"Because they know—rather, knew—Imelda." I held my cup up for a refill.

Patty nodded. "They'll be looking into every aspect of her life, I imagine."

I knew she was thinking about how the police had dredged up her life with Gregory when he'd been murdered. I opened my mouth to remind her that we both had strong alibis for the time of Imelda's death—we'd been talking to each other over the phone the entire way home—but instead of speaking, I took another bite of toast. Patty didn't need to be thinking of alibis or of Imelda lying on her grass in the cool evening air—of someone attacking the poor woman with a crowbar.

"What will you do about the play now?" Mom asked. "Will you postpone it?"

"I suppose we'll have to." Patty ran a hand across her forehead. "The play was scheduled to premiere next Friday. How could we ever get an actress to learn the part on such short notice?"

"Imelda didn't have an understudy?" Mom asked.

"No."

"Wait," I said. "The role of Mrs. Banks isn't that big of a part. In fact, we could get someone an earpiece and feed her the lines, if necessary."

"But who?" Patty asked.

I looked at Mom.

"What?" she asked.

"You'd do a great job, and you know it." I smiled slightly. "How many times have you watched the film version of *Barefoot in the Park*?"

"That's not the point," Mom said. "I don't want to take over a dead woman's role. That would be…unseemly."

"What would be unseemly is the amount of money the theater will lose if they have to go back and reprint all those posters, flyers, and programs," I said.

"We'd still have to reprint the programs," Patty said. "But I can add a dedication to Imelda in the new ones."

I finished my toast, took a last drink of coffee, and scooted my chair back from the table. "Talk her into it, Patty. I've got to get to work." I kissed Mom on the cheek. "Thanks for breakfast." With a nod at Popcorn who was sitting in the corner licking its paws, I added, "And everything."

"You're welcome." She squeezed my hand. "Be careful today."

"I'm careful every day."

I was unboxing a set of *Claiming Victory* Blu-ray discs with covers signed by the movie's director, Herman McManus. Since the movie had been shot here—the event that had brought me back home to Skillet Ridge prior to my decision to return here full- time—both locals and tourists were eager to scoop up *Claiming Victory* memorabilia.

Herman was a good guy. I made a mental note to give him a call soon to see how he was doing.

My front door gave an automatic ding dong as someone entered the shop.

Turning, I said, "Welcome to Lights, Camera, Action."

It was Detective Tilson, the law enforcement officer who had worked Gregory's homicide case. During that time, I had found her to be competent and professional.

"Am I right in thinking you aren't here to browse?" I asked.

"You are." She gazed around the store to ensure we were alone. "Is there anyone who could watch your shop while we chat?"

"My only part-time employee is Cassie, and she's in class at the community college this morning. I don't mind locking up for a few minutes though."

"I appreciate that. I'll make this as quick as possible."

I locked the door, affixed a sticky note to it saying I'd be back in approximately 15 minutes from the current time, and led Detective Tilson to the backroom that served as my office and storage space.

Taking a seat at my desk, I waited until Detective Tilson had also sat before asking, "Is this about Imelda?"

"Yes." She drew her brows together. "Have you spoken with your sister?"

"Not since breakfast this morning at our mom's house. We received word from a paramedic last night that the poor woman had been murdered with a crowbar. The paramedic is in the production of *Barefoot in the Park*, as was Imelda." I shrugged. "It wasn't hard to connect the dots that you would want to speak with me about Imelda since I was at the play rehearsal last night. Plus, I desperately hope hers is the only murder you're currently investigating."

"It is, but don't be so naive as to think Mrs. Marshall's is presently the only suspicious death in Skillet Ridge."

"Sadly, I don't believe any of us feel safe leaving our doors unlocked anymore," I said. "What questions do you have for me?"

"Did you take notice of Imelda Marshall at the theater last night?"

"I did."

"And how was she behaving?" Detective Tilson asked.

"If you've spoken with my sister, she might have mentioned this to you but I called Patty after the rehearsal and asked what was going on between Imelda, Alfred, and Phil." I told the detective I'd observed Imelda and Phil flirting even though Imelda had arrived with Alfred. I also told her about my conversation with Patty and that Billy had later clarified the relationship between Imelda and Alfred for me.

Leaning forward in my chair and placing my forearms on the desk, I continued, "I can't understand why Imelda was out in her yard at that time of night. Did she have a dog? Had she been out walking? If so, why? She must have been looking for something."

"Those are a few of the questions we're also seeking answers to," Detective Tilson said. "Did Ms. Marshall and Mr. Dunlop seem to be arguing when they left the theater?"

"No, but they were treating each other a little coolly, which is why I thought it was weird that they were leaving together. I thought maybe Alfred and Imelda were married. You know, an older couple arriving together." I shrugged. "I suppose they could've merely been friends and that it's possible Alfred didn't care that Imelda and Phil had been flirting with each other all evening."

"Speculation does no one any good," she said. "I'm only interested in the facts. I appreciate your help, Ms. Merrill. Should you think of anything that might be relevant, please let me know."

"I will." I felt a smidge put out at her chastising me for being so curious. I couldn't help that my love of mystery movies had turned me into an armchair detective.

As I walked with Detective Tilson back to the front door and unlocked it, I wondered again why Imelda had been out in her front yard so late, who had attacked her, what had motivated her murder, and what the nosy neighbor who called 9-1-1 had actually seen. I crumpled up the sticky note and tossed it into the trash. I knew how to get at least one of those questions answered.

Chapter Four

A customer, who'd just bought one of the signed *Claiming Victory* disks, and I were talking about the movie when Billy came into the shop. He patiently walked around the store looking at merchandise he'd seen dozens of times while he waited for the customer to leave.

When she'd gone, he came over and rested his elbows on the glass-topped counter. "What do you know?"

That I'll have to clean that countertop after you leave, I thought. "Not much."

He blew out a breath and placed his chin in his palms. "Me either. I hate that Imelda was attacked like that, but...well, you know...we've put a lot of work into the play."

"I know. I believe Patty is going to address the issue tonight at the theater."

Cassie walked into the shop in time to hear the last part of my sentence. "She is. I just got a text from her."

As if on cue, Billy's phone dinged. He looked at the screen. "That's from her. We're supposed to meet at the regular time."

"Are you going to be there, Dina?" Cassie asked.

"I'm going to do my best." I smiled. "Don't worry. Everything will work out."

Billy and Cassie spoke softly for a few minutes while she dusted the shelves and items on display.

I went into my office to check my email. I'd received notification from Barry that he'd sent the script to me by express mail and that he'd insured the package. I tried to track delivery, but I was unable to do so. Hopefully, the script would be here tomorrow.

The doorbell let me know that someone had either entered or left the shop. I knew Cassie would come to get me if a customer had questions or needed something she couldn't find. However, I realized what I'd heard had been Billy leaving the shop when Cassie came into the office and perched on the chair in front of my desk.

"Is everything okay?" I asked.

"Yeah. Billy and I were talking about what happened to Imelda." She bit her lip. "Why would someone hurt her like that?"

"I don't know. It's possible that it was a random attack, that the person intended to rob her." I sighed. "I did wonder about the relationships between Imelda, Alfred, and Phil last night."

"You don't think Alfred or Phil would k—" She couldn't bring herself to say the word. "—harm Imelda, do you?"

"No." I *did* think one of them might've harmed her, but I had no real motive for either of them, and I really hated to think one of those seemingly sweet old guys had clobbered Imelda with a crowbar because she didn't return his affections.

"Me either. They're nice, and they both liked Imelda."

I contemplated her drawn face. "If it's that you're afraid to return to the theater until this situation is resolved—"

"I'm not." She brought her chin up resolutely. "Not at all."

"Okay. But if you change your mind, you'll tell me, won't you?"

"Sure," she said, managing a weak smile. "I'm all right—just shaken up over this whole thing."

"So am I. We all are."

After work, I went by the bakery and bought an apple pie for Imelda's neighbor. Billy had given me the address after I'd told him I wanted to check on the lady who'd called 9-1-1 for Imelda. The house wasn't terribly far from Lights, Camera, Action.

When I pulled into the woman's driveway, I saw the curtain move. Clearly, she or someone who lived with her was peeping out. I lifted my hand in a friendly wave, carefully picked up the pie, and got out of the car. I walked to the door and rang the bell.

I was standing on the stoop contemplating whether or not I should ring the bell again when the woman cracked open the door and peered at me. I could hear a small dog barking from inside the house.

"What is it you want?" she said, her voice reminding me of a frog's croak.

"I'm Dina Merrill. I was acquainted with Imelda Marshall, and I understand you're the one who called 9-1-1 when you noticed Imelda lying on her front lawn. I wanted to stop by and make sure you're okay."

She crooked a finger toward the pie box. "What's that?"

"Apple pie. It's a thank you for caring about your neighbor. These days too many people only care about themselves."

"That's true." The woman's shaggy brows drew together. "I'm calling my daughter to tell her you're here, and then I'll let you come inside."

"All right." I waited while the woman took a photo of me and one of the car, sent the pictures to her daughter, and then called the daughter and gave her my name.

"She thinks I'm paranoid, but I'm a woman living alone. I think it's wise to take precautions." She opened the door and allowed me to enter her home.

Once I was allowed inside, the dog—a tiny creature that appeared to be a cross between a Yorkshire terrier and a Chihuahua—decided I must be all right. While it didn't jump up to be petted, it did stop barking.

I looked around the tidy living room. The woman had a sofa that looked as if it was seldom used, a wingback chair, and a recliner that appeared to be her favorite seat. There was a small table beside the recliner that held a crossword puzzle book, a small round container filled with pens, some dog treats, a skein of green yarn, and a pair of knitting needles.

"I absolutely agree," I said. "After all, look at poor Imelda."

"That's right." She motioned for me to follow her to the kitchen where she put a pot of coffee on to percolate.

The dog followed the woman into the kitchen and hopped around yipping at the two of us.

I placed the pie onto the table while the woman took out two dessert plates, two forks, and a pie server.

"Here." She opened the back door and allowed the dog to go outside. She turned back to me. "I'm Mary."

"It's a pleasure to meet you. I'm sorry it's under these circumstances, though."

"So am I. Imelda was a tolerable neighbor. We weren't on bad terms or anything, but I didn't agree with her dating and trying to be an actress and that sort of nonsense. I felt that behavior was unseemly for a woman of her age."

The coffee finished percolating, and Mary filled two cups with the aromatic dark roast.

"Shall I cut the pie?" I asked.

"Please. Sugar and cream?"

"Yes, please."

Mary nodded thoughtfully. "You appear to be a sensible young woman. What do you do?"

I gave Mary the biggest slice of the pie, figuring my good assessment in her eyes was about to take a dive. "I own a movie memorabilia shop in town."

"So you're a businesswoman?"

"That's right."

"You don't go in for any of that silly acting yourself, do you?" she asked.

"No, ma'am."

"Good." She took a bite of her pie. "This is tasty. The crust isn't as flaky as mine, but the filling is nice. I'll give you my apple pie recipe before you leave."

"I'd appreciate that very much." I was wondering how I was going to maneuver the conversation back around to Imelda and who might've wanted to harm her. I needn't have worried.

"Did Imelda ever come to your shop?"

"No, I don't believe she ever did," I said.

"I'm surprised. She had some autographs and things like that. You might talk with her grandson about it." She gestured with her fork. "Now there's a wonderful boy. Handsome too. About your age."

"What's his name?"

"Kurt. He's thoughtful, like you. He'd always volunteer to do lawn work for me or clean out my gutters. And he never would take a penny for doing it." She scraped her chair back from the table, got up, and left the room. When she returned, she handed me a business card. "This is his. I have more than one. You should call him."

"I will," I said. "I'd like to express my condolences, and I'm sure my mother and sister will as well."

Mary sat back down and resumed eating her pie.

"Was it unusual for Imelda to be outside at night?" I asked.

She shrugged. "I never knew what to expect from that woman. She often came in late after going on one of her dates."

"Right. Do you think it was one of her dates who hit her on the head? Or was she maybe in the wrong place at the wrong time—looking for a pet or something—when some random burglar came along?"

"I have no idea," Mary said. "I don't even know whether or not she had any pets. If she did, they didn't bother me, which is a mark in her favor."

"Did the police talk with you?" I asked.

"Of course, they did. I found her. They asked all these questions about what I saw and if I'd noticed anything suspicious." She sipped her coffee. "Yes, I saw something suspicious! I saw Imelda sprawled out in her front yard, and she wasn't moving! Is there any circumstance where that *wouldn't* be suspicious?"

"No." I pitied poor Detective Tilson if she was the person who'd questioned Mary. "Are you all right by yourself? I could drive you to your daughter's house if you're afraid to stay here after what happened to your neighbor."

"You're a sweet girl. I'll put in a good word for you with Kurt. But, no, dear, my daughter lives in Louisiana."

"Oh. Still—if you're afraid—"

"I'm not. Don't you worry about me. Skippy and I are fine. We stay close to the house, and we can rely on Bertha if need be."

"Bertha?"

She nodded at something behind my head.

I turned and noticed a 12-gauge shotgun on a rack hanging on the wall behind me. "Wow. Bertha is…um…intimidating."

"You'd better believe she is."

At least, Mary could be ruled out as a suspect. She wouldn't have hit Imelda with a crowbar. She'd have unleashed Bertha on her.

I turned back to Mary, who was finishing off her slice of pie.

"Thank you for this," she said. "You're a thoughtful young lady."

"You're welcome." I looked at my watch. "I really need to get home. It's been a pleasure meeting you."

"Likewise. You be careful now. You never know who or what might be lurking around."

"Right."

As I left, I saw the curtains move as I had when I'd arrived. She was watching me. Was it to make sure I made it to the car okay, or was it because she was still suspicious of me?

Chapter Five

I opened the door to Mom's house and was greeted by the comforting aroma of meatloaf. "It smells great in here."

"Thanks, hon. As soon as Patty mashes the potatoes, we can eat."

"Where've you been?" Patty jabbed the potato masher into the cubed potatoes and added a bit more cream.

"I paid a visit to Imelda's neighbor, Mary." I dropped my handbag onto a chair. "She didn't seem to care much for Imelda, but she says she didn't see anything suspicious last night—other than Imelda lying immobile on her front lawn."

"Is she a suspect?" Mom asked, setting out plates, silverware, and napkins.

"I rather doubt it. She appears to be older than Imelda, and I don't think she'd have the strength to hit someone with a crowbar hard enough to do much more than leave a bruise. Besides, why use a crowbar when Bertha would be more efficient?"

"Bertha?" Patty asked. "Is that her dog?"

"No, it's her shotgun."

Mom straightened, eyes wide. "Did she threaten you with Bertha?"

"No, Mom." I smiled. "In fact, I think she liked me. At least, she thought I was nice enough to warrant an introduction to Imelda's grandson, Kurt."

Turning her mouth down at the corners, Mom said, "I wouldn't exactly call that a meet-cute, but at this point, I'll take it."

I detoured around that subject. "Mary said Imelda had some celebrity autographs. Did Imelda ever talk with you about that, Patty?"

"She did. I don't know the provenance of the photo or anything, but she was certainly proud of her signed Robert Redford portrait." She finished the potatoes. "Rather than transfer these to a serving bowl, I'm just going to spoon them out of the mixing bowl. One less dish to wash."

Taking three glasses from the cabinet, I asked, "Mom, how did the flyers turn out?"

"Flyers?" Mom didn't meet my eyes.

"Yes. For the cat."

"Oh, that. I didn't make it into town today." She glanced at Popcorn who was curled up on the sofa. "I didn't want to go off and leave the poor thing. What if I came home and the cat was missing from here? Then anyone responding to the flyer would be getting their hopes up for nothing."

"Uh-huh." I placed the glasses on the table.

"Seriously! Wouldn't that be awful?" She was trying so hard to look earnest that it was all I could do not to laugh.

"It would be." When I noticed that Patty was pressing her lips together in a desperate attempt to keep from giggling, that made my own laughter bubble up and spill out.

Patty and Mom joined in. I believe it was the stress reliever we all needed.

"Mom, you were adamant that you were not going to take care of a cat when I brought Popcorn in here yesterday," I reminded her.

"Yes, but that's before I got to know the little sweetheart." She sighed. "I don't want to keep someone else's cat, but—well, I hope no one claims him. I believe he's happy here."

We finished up dinner, tidied the kitchen, and then Patty and I drove together to the theater.

At the theater, the cast and crew gathered anxiously, everyone obviously on edge over what had happened to Imelda and the fate of the play they'd been working so hard to get ready to perform.

Patty cleared her throat, clutching her hands tightly together. "I know the police have already spoken with all of you about the attack on Imelda. In light of this situation, I want to discuss whether we should continue with the production or postpone it."

A murmur of concern and sadness rippled through the room.

"I'm devastated by the loss of my dear friend," Alfred said, "but she wouldn't want us to give up on this production."

"I agree," Cassie said. "But Imelda's character is vital to the plot. How are we going to find someone on such short notice to adequately replace her?"

"I might have a solution," Patty said. "My mom is a huge Robert Redford fan, and she's seen the movie *Barefoot in the Park* about a million times."

"Imelda was also a Robert Redford devotee." Alfred blinked back tears. "She was ever so proud of the signed photograph of the actor taken during a scene from *Butch Cassidy and the Sundance Kid*. She'd met Mr. Redford at a charity gala she attended with her parents at the Waldorf Astoria in 1970."

"I'd love to see that photo," I said, unable to help myself.

Patty shot me a look that said this wasn't the time nor the place and said, "I understand the challenges we're facing, but Alfred is right—Imelda would want the show to go on. Let's honor her by putting on the best performance we can and dedicating the show to her and to raising awareness about the importance of safety in our community."

Everyone began speaking at once, fully in agreement with Patty's suggestion.

I noticed Phil Lemon was sitting a bit apart from everyone else and was looking down at the floor. I went over to speak with him.

"Phil, are you all right?"

He raised his head. "Yeah. I'm fine. Sad about Imelda, that's all. Seems like I'm about the only one more concerned about her than the play."

"That's not true. We're all sad about Imelda. But we can't bring her back. We can only hope to get justice for her and to honor her by putting on the best play we possibly can without her."

Patty dismissed the cast and crew then, saying she'd see them all back there tomorrow evening for a full rehearsal.

"Do you really believe your mom can pull this off?" Cassie asked.

"If anyone can, she can," Patty said. "I'll take her a script and get her started on memorizing her lines."

When I got home, I placed my handbag on the table by the door, took off my shoes, and stretched out on the sofa. Noticing something sticking out of my pocket, I pulled out the business card Mary had given me.

Kurt Marshall, Heirloom Antiques

I debated for a few moments about whether or not to call. Would it seem weird for a stranger to call out of the blue? Yes, but it might not be so bad once I explained how I'd gotten his number. Plus, he might know if his grandmother had any enemies or had expressed fear of someone. Still, I should probably wait until working hours. But if I did, he might be too busy to speak with me. I could call, very quickly say I'm sorry for his loss, and end the conversation. Unless he gave me information about who he believed would want to kill his grandmother.

Holding my breath, I tapped the numbers on my phone's keypad, exhaled, and pressed the *call* icon.

The phone rang a couple of times, and I was on the verge of hanging up when a deep, smooth voice said, "Hello, this is Kurt Marshall."

"Hi, Kurt. My name is Dina Merrill. I knew your grandmother, and I'm calling to say I'm so very sorry for your loss."

"Um...thank you." He sounded cautious and curious.

"I got your name and number from Mary, Imelda's neighbor," I said quickly. "I went to see her today to check on her because—well, you know."

"She found Gran," he said.

"Right. I thought she might be frightened, but—"

He chuckled. "Not Mary. She's one tough old lady. She and Gran didn't always see eye to eye, but I believe Mary will miss her. How did you know Gran?"

"I'm the set designer for Skillet Ridge Repertory Theater. My sister, Patty, is the manager."

"Of course," he said. "Gran was really looking forward to appearing in that play."

"I know. I'm so sorry."

"Thank you, Dina. I appreciate your call and your kind words. It's been a difficult time for our family."

"I can only imagine," I said. "If there's anything I can do to help or support you and your family during this time, please don't hesitate to let me know. I didn't know Imelda as well as I'd have liked, but she seemed to be an incredible woman."

"She was. Thanks again." He paused. "You said you're the set designer?"

"That's right."

"How did the other people on set behave toward Gran?"

"She got along great with everyone," I said. "In fact, I thought at first that she and Alfred were married."

"I've met Alfred. He came across as a stand-up guy to me."

"I think he is too."

"Is the play still going forward?" he asked.

"Um…it is. They're planning to dedicate it to Imelda." Did he think that was in poor taste, or did he understand that it was in the best interest of the theater and the other performers that the show proceed as planned?

"Nice. I'd like to come by and watch the next rehearsal. Would that be all right?" His tone was guarded.

"I don't know why it wouldn't be," I said. "It's tomorrow evening at six p.m."

"I'll be there. Thanks, Dina."

"You're welcome. I look forward to meeting you in person, although I certainly wish it was under different circumstances."

"Yeah, me, too."

I wondered if Kurt was suspicious of someone in the cast or crew. After all, it was following play rehearsal that Imelda was attacked. Had Imelda voiced concerns to Kurt about someone in the cast or crew? Was there something she'd known about one of them that got her killed?

Chapter Six

Both the phone I'd ordered for *Barefoot in the Park* and a package from Barry arrived the next morning. Although I was eager to open them both, especially the one from Barry, I was with a customer who was buying a reprint of the movie poster for *The Hound of the Baskervilles*. She was gushing about how much she loved Sherlock Holmes and all the actors who've played him—from Basil Rathbone to Benedict Cumberbatch to Johnny Lee Miller to Henry Cavill.

"Am I missing anyone?" she asked.

Despite wanting to finish the transaction so I could open the box containing the *Casablanca* script I'd been waiting for so anxiously, I couldn't possibly let her forget

Robert Downey, Junior. I reminded my customer of the movies starring Downey and Jude Law.

"Oh my gosh!" she exclaimed. "How could I ever forget Robert Downey, Junior?"

I laughed. "Well, there have been a lot of Sherlock Holmes...Holmeses? Maybe I should make a collage of all the actors who've portrayed the famous detective."

"Absolutely you should," she said.

I put that on my mental to-do list and wished her a good day as she left with her framed poster.

As the customer was driving away, I slipped on a pair of white cotton gloves and removed the script from the box. There was also a sheet of paper with the provenance of the script. This was one of the scripts titled *Everybody Comes to Rick's*. Although it had been shopped around to studios, the script wasn't bought until the name was changed to *Casablanca*. This script was truly a piece of movie history.

I was so engrossed in reading the script that I started when the electronic doorbell chimed alerting me that someone had entered the shop. It was Liza, the mail carrier.

"Hi, Dina! It's a nice day out there. Hope you get a chance to enjoy it!"

"So do I." I turned the script face down in the box and removed my gloves. "Has anyone on your route mentioned that they've lost a cat?"

"No. I'm guessing you found one?"

"Yes. White with some yellow markings." I took out my phone and showed her a photo I'd taken.

"It looks familiar."

"If I print out a few copies of this photo, would you mind taking them with you to see if anyone on your delivery circuit lost him?" I asked. "I plan on going to the print shop after work, but if you see anyone on your route looking for him, that would be a lot more expedient."

She hesitated. "I'd love to, but I've probably been here too long already. Our deliveries are timed, and if I get behind in my route, I'll get in trouble."

"I understand."

"I'll be happy to pick up a few of the flyers you make when I come by here in the morning, though."

"That'd be great," I said. "Thank you."

When Liza left, I put my gloves back on and removed the script from the box. This time, the script was turned over, and I noticed a small, faded, handwritten inscription in the bottom left corner.

We'll always have Paris, Imelda. Love, R

My eyes widened as an icy chill jolted though my body. "Imelda?" It couldn't be. Could it?

It had to be a coincidence. But what if it wasn't?

Once again, I returned the script to the box and carried the box into my office. Removing my gloves, I took out my phone and texted Barry.

Just got the script, and it looks fantastic. By the way, what was the name of the family from whom you bought the script?

He immediately texted back, *Turner. Why do you want to know?*

I wrote back telling him about the inscription. *It wouldn't be so weird except that a woman named Imelda was murdered here in Skillet Ridge a couple of nights ago.*

Totally weird, but totally a coincidence, he texted.

Yeah. Still kinda spooky. I inserted a smile emoji. *Anyway, thanks again for acquiring this for me. Please keep an eye out for more goodies.*

He said he would and promised to come visit the shop one of these days.

As I put my phone away, I wondered if it really was just a coincidence. Probably. But still…. I wished I could call Kurt and tell him what I'd found, but I doubted it was the right time. His family was likely busy getting Imelda's memorial service planned, and I didn't want to intrude on their grief.

I put the gloves back on and started back at the beginning, reading the script. Although I was delighted to see some of my favorite lines from the movie, my discovery of the inscription had put a slight damper on my enthusiasm.

That evening was hectic. I went to the printers after work and had twenty-five flyers made, grabbed a quick bite at a fast-food restaurant, and then hurried on to the theater.

As the cast and crew gathered for the rehearsal, I noticed a handsome but unfamiliar face standing near the entrance. Could it be Kurt? He'd mentioned that he might come to the theater, but I hadn't actually expected him to do so.

Taking a deep breath, I walked over to the man, suddenly feeling as nervous as a middle school girl at a Sadie Hawkins dance. "Are you Kurt?"

He smiled. "I am. Dina, right? Thank you for your kind words on the phone. It's comforting to know my grandmother had such good people in her life."

"Again, I'm so sorry for your loss," I said.

Kurt sighed and ran a hand through his hair. "I can't believe she's gone. It's been tough on our family, but I'm determined to find out what happened to her."

"It's the strangest thing. I came across an original *Casablanca* script today, and there's an inscription on the back that mentions an Imelda. I know it's ridiculous, but I couldn't help but wonder if your grandmother could be that Imelda."

"I wouldn't say it's out of the realm of possibility," he said. "Gran was involved with a lot of film clubs and went to a lot of movie events when she was living in New York. Do you have the script with you?"

"No, it's at my shop, but I'd be happy to show it to you later."

"I'd appreciate that. Are you free tomorrow evening? We could meet at my grandmother's house." He smiled. "I know you'll enjoy seeing some of her movie memorabilia."

"That would be great." I jerked my head toward the cast. "Come on over and meet everyone."

Kurt followed me over to the stage.

"Excuse me, everyone," I said. "I'm sorry to interrupt, but I'd like to introduce you to Kurt Marshall, Imelda's grandson."

Raising his hand in a quick wave, Kurt said, "Hi. I just wanted to invite all of you to Gran's memorial service. It'll be at four o'clock tomorrow afternoon at Skillet Ridge Baptist Church. And…um…thank you for being such an important part of Gran's life."

Alfred, who had already met Kurt, approached him with a warm smile and extended his arms for a hug. "Kurt, good to see you again. I adored your grandmother, and I already miss her terribly."

"Thank you, Alfred," Kurt said. "That means a lot. Imelda spoke highly of you."

"Ah, you were the apple of her eye, my boy." Alfred brushed away tears.

The rest of the cast and crew approached Kurt one by one, expressing their condolences and offering their support. They shared stories about Imelda and expressed their gratitude for the opportunity to work with her. All except Phil. He disappeared backstage.

I decided to see what in the world was the matter with him. As I stormed backstage to confront Phil about his bad behavior, I saw the side door close. I followed Phil into the alley, but I wasn't fast enough. He was gone.

Chapter Seven

On Saturday morning, Cassie and I were working on a window display showcasing the movie *James and the Giant Peach.* Cassie's dad had helped with the construction of the peach, and we'd obtained an enormous fuzzy spider from a party supply store.

"She needs a beret," Cassie said of the spider.

The front door alarm chimed, and I automatically said, "Welcome to Lights, Camera, Action. Thank you for coming in. May we help you find anything in particular?"

"Just browsing," a man's voice answered.

I stood and dusted off my jeans. "If you need our assistance, please let us know."

"I will." The man was older, thin, and had a shock of white hair. "Nice collection you have here."

"Thank you."

"You look familiar," Cassie told him. "Did you visit the Skillet Ridge Repertory Theater last week?"

"I did." His tone was dismissive at first, but then he elaborated. "I was there visiting a friend. I'm in town today for her memorial."

I didn't recall seeing the man myself. He must have been at the theater on a night I'd been absent.

"You must mean Imelda," I said.

"I do indeed." He nodded toward a nearby display case. "You have a nice collection here."

"Thank you." I wanted to ask how he knew Imelda, but I didn't want to be intrusive. I was glad when he decided to elaborate on their relationship.

"Imelda and I were members of the same film club when we were living in New York. She moved back many years ago, of course, but we kept in touch through club correspondence. My wife and I moved to East Tennessee a while back, so I thought it would be nice to visit Southwest Virginia and reconnect with Imelda now and again." He sighed. "Unfortunately, the two of us didn't get much of an opportunity to do that."

"What a shame," I said.

"Where's your wife?" Cassie asked.

"She's ill and wasn't up to making the trip today," the man said.

"I'm sorry to hear that." I walked over to the counter as Cassie put the finishing touches on the display, with the exception of the spider's beret. I was certain I had one at home that would fit the bill nicely.

"That's really cool that you were in a film club in New York." Cassie straightened and smiled at the man. "Did you get to meet a lot of celebrities?"

"A few," he said. "Not as many as you might think, but some. We went to a number of premieres, staged some retro events, had some screenings, panel discussions, and things like that. It was fun. I enjoy knowing the story behind the story."

"That sounds fantastic," I said.

"Yes, well, I'm sure you feel the same way or else you wouldn't have this shop," he said.

"I do love having as much of the behind-the-scenes information as possible." I smiled. "It makes the movie that much richer to me."

"What was Imelda's favorite movie?" Cassie asked.

"You were in the play together, weren't you?" The man frowned. "I'd have imagined she'd have talked with you about movies all the time."

"Actually, she didn't. We didn't socialize all that much during our rehearsals. We didn't even know she had a signed photograph of Robert Redford until…" She hesitated. "Until recently."

Neither Cassie nor Billy paid much attention to anyone else during their time at the theater, but that was understandable.

He smiled sadly. "Redford was her favorite actor, but her favorite movie had to have been *Casablanca*."

I opened my mouth to ask about the inscription I'd found on the script I'd acquired, but I thought better of it. I wanted to know more about this man before I trusted him enough to ask him very many questions about Imelda.

"So, you'll be at Imelda's memorial service this afternoon, Mr.—?" I prompted.

"Flax." He nodded. "Yes, I'll be there."

"Well, my name is Dina, and this is Cassie."

Cassie gave him a little wave. "Did you and your wife ever perform?"

He shrugged. "We both did some community theater, and we worked as extras in a film or two no one's ever heard of."

"Cool." She grinned.

"It was indeed cool. Thank you, ladies, for letting me browse. I might come in again before I head back home. And it's likely I'll see you at the memorial service." He gave us a nod and left.

"That was odd," I said, after he left. "He came up here last week to talk with Imelda, and then drove back here today and has—" I checked my watch. "—six hours before the memorial service begins. That doesn't make sense. Why would he be here so early?"

"If his wife was too sick to make the trip, why come at all?" Cassie asked.

"Did he and Imelda seem particularly chummy when they spoke at the theater?"

"No. In fact, she seemed uncomfortable that he was there."

"Maybe he knows the Marshall family." Trying to put the man out of my mind and concentrate on my work, I went to take another look at the display. "I think this looks great. Do you mind going outside to see what it looks like from the sidewalk?"

Cassie went home early to get ready for Imelda's memorial service, but I got involved in my work and let time slip away from me. As a result, I had to go straight from Lights, Camera, Action! to the chapel. I was in such a rush that I accidentally left the "Found Cat" flyers on the counter by the cash register—not that I'd have had time to distribute them anyway.

I hurried to the chapel, stood outside the door for a moment to catch my breath and steady my nerves, and then went inside. I spotted Patty in the line waiting to greet the family and offer condolences. She tried to wave me over, but I shook my head slightly not wanting to get ahead of those who'd been standing in line.

Glancing around, I saw other familiar faces: Cassie and her dad, Billy, Artie, the man who'd visited the shop this morning—Mr. Flax, he'd said. I didn't see Phil, and I didn't see Mom. Mom might've stayed home with the cat.

I felt a pang of guilt over not distributing the flyers and especially over not particularly wanting to do so. Mom really liked Popcorn, and he was good company for her.

Someone stepped up behind me, and I turned to see Phil. He had his hands in his pockets, and he looked as if he'd rather be anywhere else. Of course, no one *wanted* to attend a memorial service.

"How are you?" I asked.

"Good as can be expected, I guess. Horrible thing about Imelda."

"It is. Had you known her before you started working on the play together?"

"Not well," he said. "I mean, I'd seen her around— knew who she was. I got to know her fairly well while we worked on the play."

"Yeah. I wish I'd known her better." I smiled sadly. "It seems she and I would've had a lot we could've talked about given her interest in movies. There was a man in my shop this morning who said he and his wife had been in a film club with Imelda in New York several years ago."

"Who was the guy?" he asked.

"The white-haired man up there in the blue shirt. He's behind the lady in the black dress."

He snorted. "Reggie Flax. Figures."

"You know him?"

"I've seen him at the theater a time or two. I don't trust the guy."

The line was moving, so I merely gave Phil a quick nod and turned to take a couple steps forward. I stood quietly looking down at the memorial card in my hands thinking about what Phil had said. Was he mistaken in thinking Mr. Flax had been to the theater more than once? If not, why had Mr. Flax been so insistent on visiting with Imelda; and why had he felt the need to lie about it to Cassie and me?

At last, I was at the front of the line. Fortunately, Kurt was the first family member I saw.

"Hi, Kurt. I'm so sorry for your loss."

"Thank you." He introduced me to his parents.

I expressed my condolences to them and then moved on to take a seat on a pew with Patty, Cassie, and Billy.

Patty clasped my hand. "Thanks for coming."

"I wish I had known Imelda better," I said.

I didn't mention to Patty that Kurt and I planned to go to Imelda's house after the memorial service and brief reception at his parents' house. Who knew whether or not we'd uncover anything promising that could lead to the identity of Imelda's killer, and I didn't want to get her hopes up. I also didn't want her telling Mom, who wouldn't want me poking my nose into another murder investigation. Visiting a man's dead grandmother's house to look for clues definitely did not fall under Mom's definition of a "meet-cute."

It was nearly nine o'clock that night by the time Kurt and I arrived at Imelda's house. It felt eerie to me, going into her home and looking at her belongings knowing she'd never be back.

There were framed photographs of Kurt going several years back. He caught me looking at his high-school graduation portrait and blushed. I smiled. There were black-and-white photographs of a young boy who looked a lot like Kurt, so I knew they must be of his dad. There were also photos of Kurt's parents, Kurt with both his parents and Imelda, and an older photo of Imelda and a man who I thought must be her husband.

I followed Kurt into a small room Imelda had turned into a library or study. It was there that the framed, autographed still of Robert Redford from the movie *Butch Cassidy and the Sundance Kid* was proudly displayed.

"That's fantastic," I said.

"Yeah. She loved Bob Redford." He chuckled. "Here's how she always told the story: 'I met Bob Redford when I was a mere seventeen years old. What a dashing figure of a man he was.' She and her parents were at some sort of charity gala."

"I'm so glad he was nice to her and made the event such a memorable occasion for her," I said.

"Yeah, she certainly carried that memory with her forever." He sat down behind the desk and opened up a drawer. "I'm eager to see what else she might have in here. I realize that what happened to Gran might have been a random act of violence, but it doesn't feel that way. It feels personal to me. Otherwise, why didn't her attacker come inside and rob the house?"

I wasn't at ease rifling through Imelda's personal belongings, but I did peruse the titles of some of the books on her shelf. She had several books on Hollywood lore, biographies, memoirs, and tell-alls. She also had movie magazines that spanned several decades.

"Look at this."

Turning at the sound of Kurt's voice, I went over to the desk to see what he'd found. "What is it?"

He held up a leather notebook embossed on the front with the words, *"Round Up the Usual Suspects."*

"Is it a diary?" I asked.

"Maybe. I'm going to take it home with me and read through it." He stifled a yawn. "Do you work tomorrow?"

"No."

"I'd really like to see that script you were telling me about. Do you think we could meet up and take a look at it?"

"Sure," I said. "We could meet at my shop around twelve-thirty or one o'clock tomorrow afternoon."

"Twelve-thirty would be great," he said. "If I find anything interesting in this notebook, I'll bring it too."

"Sounds good." I hoped that together Kurt and I could find some answers as to who might have wanted to hurt his grandmother. And I certainly wasn't averse to spending more time with the man.

Chapter Eight

Although it was late, there were lights on at Mom's house when I drove up. Rather than going straight to the apartment, I stopped in to check on her and Patty. The two of them and Popcorn were sitting in the living room. I slumped on a chair, and Popcorn came over to hop onto my lap.

"Hello," I said, rubbing a hand gently over the cat's back.

He began to purr.

"Mom, I'm sorry, but I didn't have time to distribute the *Found Cat* flyers today. I barely made it to the memorial on time."

"I noticed," Patty said. "I was beginning to worry."

"Sorry—the day got hectic. Anyway, I'll post the flyers either tomorrow or Monday."

"No rush." Mom smiled. "I know you're very busy, darling."

Uh-huh. It wasn't that she wanted to keep the cat that she was being so understanding. It wouldn't be that at all.

"Patty, did you see the white-haired guy at the memorial service?" I asked. "His name was Reggie Flax."

"I did see Mr. Flax. He came to the theater at least one time that I'm aware of."

"How did Imelda react to him? I'm asking because Cassie's account differs from the one Reggie gave us when he came into the shop today." I rubbed Popcorn under the chin. "The way he talked, he and his wife had been friends with Imelda for years and had kept up with her through their film club; but Cassie said Imelda seemed to be uncomfortable around him."

"It appeared to me that she was uncomfortable too," Patty said. "Maybe it was the surprise at seeing him at the play or the fact that he didn't bring his wife." She squinted. "I recall he tried to take her arm once or twice, and she moved away from him both times. I didn't see a woman with him this evening."

"He told Cassie and me that his wife was ill and couldn't come. And get this—he was in the shop about six hours before the service."

"That's weird."

"I agree." Mom rose from the sofa. "Anyone want some hot cocoa before bed?"

Patty and I both declined, but I took it as a hint that Mom was ready for me to leave.

"Maybe he was in love with her," Mom said, as she walked into the kitchen. "That's kind of romantic."

I rolled my eyes at Patty, and she shook her head.

"It's not romantic if he killed her, Mom," I said.

"Well, no, that wouldn't be romantic at all. Unless..." She returned with a bottle of water. "No. It wouldn't be under any circumstances."

"I thought you were having hot cocoa," Patty said.

"Not if no one else wanted any." She sat back down on the sofa and opened the bottle.

"Oh, hey," I said to Patty, "did you happen to see Mary, Imelda's neighbor, at the memorial service? I meant to look for her, but she completely slipped my mind."

"I bet she did—as soon as you looked into Imelda's grandson's gorgeous green eyes."

Pressing my lips together, I said, "Kurt isn't what made me forget about Mary."

"I've never met Mary, so I don't know if she was there or not."

"Tell me more about this man with the gorgeous eyes," Mom said.

"There's not much to tell. He and I went to Imelda's house after the service to see if we could find anything to provide a motive for her being killed. Kurt found a notebook, and since it was late, we're going to meet tomorrow at the shop to discuss it." I raised and lifted my shoulder as nonchalantly as I could. "And I'm going to show him the *Everybody Comes to Rick's* script because I found a handwritten note on the back to an 'Imelda.' I'm wondering if there's any way it could be our Imelda."

Mom clasped her hands together. "You're seeing him again tomorrow. You must've really hit it off."

"It's not like that. We're only trying to find a motive for Imelda's murder."

"Your blush says otherwise. Don't you think so, Patty?"

My sister grinned. "She's blushing all right."

"Goodnight, Popcorn." I plucked the cat off my lap, gave him a cuddle, and gave him to Mom. "I need to get some rest. You two have a good night too."

"Sweet dreams!" Mom called, as she giggled and snuggled the cat.

I really hoped no one claimed Popcorn. Mom was attached to him already. I rather liked him myself.

As I got ready for bed, I wished I'd had time to look at some of those movie magazines Imelda had. Maybe Kurt would be willing to let me borrow some of them.

An image of Kurt's handsome face gleamed in my memory. I knew Mom would love it if I'd start dating someone. Why it was so important to Mom that her daughters be paired up was beyond me. Maybe it was simply because she was such a romantic. She was even trying to get Patty interested in dating again. But after what Patty had gone through with Gregory, I didn't know when or if Patty would ever be willing to trust anyone else.

As for Kurt, he could very well be in a relationship already. Even if he wasn't, his grandmother had just been murdered. His focus was on bringing her killer to justice—as it should be. That was my focus too.

I'd been too busy in New York getting my career off the ground to seriously date anyone. It was only after I came home to Skillet Ridge to work on the set of Claiming Victory that I realized how isolated and lonely I'd become. If this so-called investigation he and I were doing would lead to a friendship between Kurt and me, that would be great. And while I wasn't ruling out a romantic relationship down the road, I'd be happy to simply be friends with him.

On Sunday morning, I slept in. Even after I got out of bed, I was still lazy. I lingered on the sofa with a cup of coffee watching the morning news. A knock on the door startled me so badly that I nearly spilled my coffee. I wasn't used to anyone visiting me.

"Who is it?" I called.

"Me," Mom answered.

I opened the door to find her standing on the stoop with a picnic basket. Stifling a yawn, I asked, "It's a little early for a picnic, isn't it?"

"Of course. This isn't for *now*. It's for your date with Kurt."

Taking the basket, I moved aside so she could come into the apartment. "I appreciate this, Mom, but it isn't a date. We're simply meeting to determine why anyone would have wanted to kill his grandmother."

"Potato, potahto."

I took the basket over to the kitchen table, sat it down, and opened it. Inside were rolls, fruit, cheese, cold cuts, cookies, a bottle of sparkling grape juice and two champagne glasses. I lifted the bottle out of the basket and raised my eyebrows at her.

"What?" she asked. "I'm sorry. I didn't have any real champagne. That'll have to do."

"It won't do at all." I placed the bottle on the table and removed the glasses from the basket. "If I take this, he'll think I'm making a pass at him."

"Sparkling grape juice does not a pass make."

I rubbed the bridge of my nose. On the one hand, I recognized her reference to the famous *Barefoot in the Park* line, "Six days does not a week make;" and I was proud of her for digging into the script to learn her part.

On the other hand, I was not about to take a picnic lunch to a…a what? A murder discussion?

"Mom." I shook my head.

She lowered her chin. "I got up early and went to all this trouble for you, and you don't appreciate it."

"I *do* appreciate it. It's wonderful. I just—"

"You'll take it then?" She lifted her head and smiled, her eyes sparkling mischievously.

"I'll take it—all except the juice. That's staying here."

"Fine. You can save it for next time." After giving me a kiss on the cheek, she left.

I went to get ready for my meeting. A meeting to which I'd arrive feeling like a Victorian-era damsel hoping my beau would buy my picnic lunch at the town fair auction.

Upon arriving at the shop, I put the red beret I'd brought onto the head of the spider in the *James and the Giant Peach* display.

Kurt came into the shop as I was standing back admiring my handiwork. "Is the picnic basket a prop too?"

"I'm afraid not. I told my mom I was coming here today, and she made this. Apparently, she's scared we'll starve while we look at an old movie script."

He smiled. "That's nice." He picked up one of the flyers I'd left on the counter. "This looks like Paco."

"What?" I frowned.

"This cat. I think it's my grandmother's."

"Oh." I swallowed my disappointment. "I found him on the side of the road Wednesday and took him to my mother's house to keep him safe until we could locate his owner. We'll go there when we're finished, and you can take him home."

Kurt shook his head. "I can go and see if it *is* Paco, but I can't take him. My apartment building doesn't allow pets. I can't take him to my parents either because my mom is allergic to cats. Do you think your mom would like to keep him?"

"Nope." I smiled. "I *know* my mom would love to keep him."

Returning my smile, he said, "I hope it's Paco then."

"Me, too." I jerked my head toward my office. "Let's take a look at the script."

He gestured toward the picnic basket. "Shall I?"

"Be my guest."

Kurt carried the picnic basket into my office and sat it on the desk.

"Let's look at the script before we eat." I took my white gloves from the top drawer before unlocking the drawer with the script. I slipped on the gloves before taking out the script and putting it on the desk between us and flipping it over to show Kurt the inscription.

"I wish he'd signed his name, rather than his initial. It could certainly be her," he said. "I mean, she used to live in New York and was involved in the film industry."

"Did the notebook tell you much?"

He opened the messenger bag he'd been carrying and took out the notebook. Grinning, he said, "I suppose I should let you handle this. You're equipped not to damage it." He held it out to me.

I took the notebook in my gloved hands and opened it. At the front of the book, written in beautiful handwriting, was: *Usual Suspects Members*. I scanned the list.

"Reggie Flax isn't on here."

"Who?" Kurt asked.

"Reggie Flax. He was at the memorial yesterday and said he knew your grandmother from a film club."

"She could've been in more than one club, I suppose."

Nodding, I turned the page. The next page was filled with symbols Kurt was unable to interpret.

"When I saw that last night, I just put the notebook up and went to bed. Who knows what on earth that means?"

"I do," I said with a smile. "That's shorthand. I once had to create a page of shorthand waiting to be transcribed for a movie prop. I'm rusty, but I think I can figure it out." I studied the symbols for a moment and then read the message aloud. "This group has been formed by those of us dedicated to proving that the doctor—no, wait, that's *director*—Randolph Gianetti, did not commit suicide but was murdered."

Chapter Nine

K urt followed me to Mom's house. As we parked in the driveway, I noticed Patty's car was missing. I hadn't heard her say anything about going anywhere today, but sometimes she needed to be alone. I could understand that.

"Hi, Mom!" I called as I walked into the house. "Kurt is with me. He wants to see Popcorn."

"Oh, sure." She stepped into the hallway with a dish towel in her hand. "I'll just be a minute."

"Mom, this is Kurt Marshall. Kurt, Anna Marie Merrill."

"Ms. Merrill, it's a pleasure to meet you." He sniffed the air. "It smells wonderful in here. Like…caramel?"

"Good nose." Mom laughed. "I'm getting ready to take a caramel apple pie out of the oven. Be right back. Popcorn is in his favorite spot on the sofa."

I didn't even have to ask Kurt if Popcorn was indeed Paco. When we walked into the living room, the cat hopped up and ran to happily greet Kurt.

"Hey, buddy. How are you?" Kurt picked the cat up, and it butted its head against his chin.

I could hear the cat purring from across the room.

"He's thrilled to see you," I said.

Mom, who was coming into the living room, abruptly stopped. "Oh. He's yours?"

"No, he belonged to my grandmother." Kurt smiled. "I was telling Dina that I can't take him because my apartment doesn't allow pets, and my mother is allergic so that rules out her and Dad. He seems happy here."

"Well, I wasn't in the market for a cat when Dina brought him in here, but I've grown quite accustomed to him. What's his name?"

"It's Paco, but Dina said you've been calling him Popcorn. I think that's a great name for his second act."

"You do?" Mom was obviously trying not to, but she looked so happy she might burst.

"I do," Kurt said, "and Gran would be delighted to know Paco—or, rather, Popcorn—landed in such a loving home. Dad and I searched for him at the house the morning after Gran's death. We thought he must've gotten out and that Gran had been looking for him when she was attacked."

"I'm so sorry. I promise I'll take good care of him." She patted Kurt's shoulder and then gestured toward the kitchen. "Would you like some warm pie and ice cream?"

"I thought you'd never ask." He placed Popcorn onto the floor, and the cat hurried over to brush against Mom's legs.

As we sat at the table enjoying the delicious caramel apple pie topped with vanilla ice cream, I said, "I wonder what our feline friend was doing so far from home."

"Where did you say you found him?" Kurt asked.

"Between my shop and here. Your grandmother's house isn't that far from where I found him, as the crow flies, but he was still a fairly long way from home."

"That's odd." Kurt dabbed his mouth with his napkin. "Gran knew he had a tendency to roam, so she was vigilant about not letting him outside. I can't imagine how he got out."

Mom patted Kurt's hand. "Thank you for letting me know. So far, he hasn't tried to leave the house, as far as I know; but I'll make sure he doesn't."

After we finished our pie and Kurt gave Popcorn another cuddle, he and I left in his SUV to go to Imelda's house.

"What are you hoping to find in the movie magazines?" he asked.

"A quick online search for Randolph Gianetti revealed that he died in 1981. If we can find information about him before he died plus any accounts of his death, then maybe we'll have a better idea of why your grandmother and her friends were so determined that his death didn't occur as it was reported."

"Okay. When we get there, I'll let you go through the magazines, and I'll look for any evidence suggesting Gran was in another film club."

I sat on the floor with film magazines piled up all around me while Kurt searched through Imelda's desk. I had one stack of magazines that mentioned Randolph Gianetti's death along with tributes. Another stack of earlier magazines mentioned his work. A third pile contained issues that ran during the correct time period but which I hadn't had a chance to check the table of contents or leaf through yet. The fourth stack were the issues I'd already concluded made no mention of Gianetti whatsoever.

Wishing I had more time to linger over the magazines, I took one from the top of the third pile. I scanned the table of contents, and there was something about that year's Sundance Film Festival. Thinking it was logical that a director would attend the festival, I flipped over to the feature. Before I could scan the article for Randolph Gianetti's name, I caught sight of a photograph. In it was a much younger Imelda Marshall. Or at least I thought it was.

"Kurt?"

"What is it?"

"I think…. Is this your grandmother?"

He came to sit on the floor beside me. "It is. Wow. Look how young she was. And she looks so pretty and happy."

"And she's with Randolph Gianetti."

"She is." He ran his hand over his mouth. "See how they're looking at each other? I think they were in love."

"So do I." I blew out a breath. "I wish there was someone we could talk with who knew your grandmother before she left New York to start her life over in Skillet Ridge."

"What about that man who was at the memorial—Reggie Flax?"

"I'm not sure we can trust him since he's not listed among the *Usual Suspects* group, but right now, he's the only lead we've got." I took out my phone, opened a popular social media app, and quickly found the correct Reggie Flax. "Here he is. Should I send him a message?"

"Please. Tell him you and I are going through Gran's movie memorabilia and that we'd like to ask him some questions about her life in New York."

I sent the message.

"I don't know how far he lives from here," Kurt said. "I don't mind going to visit him, if he can provide some of the answers we're looking for."

My phone dinged. Reggie had replied to my message.

He'd written, *As luck would have it, I'm still in town, and I'd love to talk with you. Could we meet in town at the coffee shop in half an hour?*

I raised my eyebrows at Kurt questioningly. He nodded. I wrote back to Reggie accepting his invitation.

Reggie was sitting in the corner of the coffee shop with a steaming mug of coffee when Kurt and I walked in. He waved to us, and we joined him.

"Thank you for making time for us, Mr. Flax," Kurt said. He pulled out a chair for me. "Dina, what would you like to drink?"

"I'm fine with water," I said.

"Me, too." Kurt walked away from the table and returned with two bottles of water.

"The pleasure is all mine," Reggie said, once Kurt had sat down. "I don't get to reminisce very often about those early days in New York, and I'm glad you're seeing fit to indulge an old man and his memories."

"How is your wife today?" I asked Reggie.

"She's fine." He waved away my concern with a flick of his hand. "She has a cold, that's all. Mainly, she was afraid of giving it to everyone else. That's why she didn't come."

I wasn't sure I believed that. I had so many questions about this man. Why had he come to town so early to the memorial? Had he been in Skillet Ridge already? If so, for how long? And why hadn't he left after the memorial?

Kurt's voice shook me out of my reverie. "As I'm going through Gran's belongings, I'm realizing there's a part of her life I know nothing about."

Reggie smiled, an expression filled with melancholy and wistfulness. "Ah, you should've seen her back then. I'm sure I've got some photos somewhere. I'll try to find them and scan them into the computer so I can send them to you, Kurt. She was so lovely, so vivacious, so intriguing."

Reggie had been in love with Imelda. From the expression on his face, he still was. Maybe that was the real reason his wife had refused to attend Imelda's memorial service.

Kurt and I had discussed on the way over how we'd conduct this interview. I was up.

"We found a photograph of Imelda with some director named Randolph Gianetti in one of the movie magazines. Did you know this Gianetti fellow?" I shrugged. "I know a lot about movies, but I'm afraid I'm unfamiliar with this man and his work."

"He didn't have a lot of work to be familiar with." Reggie's voice took on a slight edge. "He'd made a couple of decent films—one premiered at Sundance, that one was his biggest—but he was no Scorsese."

"From what I saw in a later issue of the magazine, he didn't live very long." I uncapped my water bottle. "Am I right that he died young?"

Nodding, Reggie said, "He died the year after that premier at Sundance. Committed suicide."

Kurt and I exchanged subtle glances. Reggie's opinion on Randolph Gianetti's death explained why he wasn't a member of the *Usual Suspects*.

"Really? That's terrible!" I took a drink of water.

"Yes, it was tragic," Reggie said. "He had everything going for him: Imelda, a career that was on the upswing—"

"What?" Kurt interrupted.

"I said the man had everything going for him."

"You said he had Imelda." Kurt leaned closer. "Was he her boyfriend?"

"More than that. The two of them were engaged." Reggie shook his head. "I don't wish to speak ill of the dead, but Gianetti didn't deserve Imelda. That man was greedy and narcissistic, but Imelda wouldn't hear anything bad about him. I tried to tell her."

"After his death," I said softly, "is that when she left New York?"

"Yep. It broke my heart to see her leave New York, but I understand why she did." His face had hardened as he spoke about Randolph Gianetti, but now he struggled to relax his features. "And it appears she built a wonderful life for herself here. I'm glad. I always wanted her to have nothing but the best."

"It sounds as if you were a good friend to her, Mr. Flax," Kurt said. "Thank you."

"I wish I could've done more—wish she'd have listened to me about Randolph. He was a playboy. He was never going to give her the life she craved. She needed stability. I—" He broke off, rubbing his forehead. "His death was the best thing that could've happened to her."

What else did Reggie Flax know about Randolph Gianetti's death? I rubbed my arms to hide the goosebumps.

Chapter Ten

After talking with Reggie, Kurt and I returned to Imelda's house. We both felt we needed more information on both Randolph Gianetti and Reggie Flax, and we hoped to contact other *Usual Suspects* members from the data Imelda had logged into the notebook.

Could Imelda's knowledge about what really happened to Randolph Gianetti have been the motive for her murder after all these years? It seemed pretty far-fetched, but then *any* reason for someone to want Imelda dead was unreasonable.

When we got out of Kurt's SUV, Mary opened her door and came outside. She must have been watching for us out her living room window.

"Is there anything I can help you do, Kurt?" she called, as she hurried toward us.

"Oh, no, thank you, Mary." He took Imelda's house key from his pocket and inserted it into the lock.

"You've always been so helpful to me. I'd love to help in any way I can." She remained standing so close that it was apparent to me that she intended on going inside with us. "I'm not as young as I used to be, but I'm still a hotshot with a broom and a mop."

Kurt opened the door, and Mary cut in front of me to follow him inside.

"We're not doing too much cleaning," Kurt said.

"Imelda was an immaculate housekeeper," I added. "There hasn't been a need to tidy up."

"Of course not, but you've been here quite a bit, so I thought you were getting the house ready to sell or something." Mary looked around the living room. "I understand Imelda had a lot of movie stuff. Are you wanting to buy it, Dina?"

"I might, if Kurt's family decides to sell any of it."

"Mary, did Gran ever talk with you about her life in New York prior to her moving here to Skillet Ridge?"

"No." She sniffed. "The two of us were very different and didn't talk very much. We were cordial, mind you, but we each had our own affairs to attend to. I need to get back home. Please do let me know if I can help you clean or anything if and when you're ready to sell the house."

"I will. Thank you, Mary." Kurt frowned at me as she walked away.

Waiting for her to leave, I said, "Mary didn't seem terribly fond of your grandmother, but she certainly likes you. She told me you helped her out a lot."

He shrugged. "I saw her struggling with her groceries one day while it was raining, helped her get everything inside, and the dye was cast."

"You're a good guy."

"I try." He jerked his head toward the study. "Shall we divide and conquer this list of names in the *Usual Suspects*?"

"Sounds good to me."

After photographing the original list with my phone, I took the first half of the list while Kurt started on the last half. For the next hour, we quietly worked on our phones to search for Imelda's film group friends.

The women were harder to find because some had possibly married or divorced since the list was originally made. One, however, had a social media account that included her maiden name. I sent her a message and hoped I'd hear back from her, as she was the only person on my list that I was able to identify as a living person who was likely the one who was part of the *Usual Suspects* group.

Kurt was even less successful. The two members he found were mentioned in separate obituaries from several years ago.

He stood, stretched, and sighed. "I'm so tired of trying to 'round up the usual suspects.' What do you say we call it quits for now? Hopefully, we'll hear from your contact tomorrow."

"Sounds good." I smiled and took the hand he offered to help me up off the floor. "I wonder if your grandmother ever mentioned to your dad that she'd once been engaged to a movie director."

"If so, he never mentioned it to me. Maybe I should talk with Mom about it first and see if she knows anything."

Kurt dropped me off in front of Mom's house. I was glad to see Patty's car in the driveway. Not that I'd been particularly anxious about her, but I had to admit I had been a little concerned. Even though she was my older sister by just under two years, I often felt protective of her.

I went inside to find Mom and Patty sitting on the sofa. Popcorn was nestled in Mom's lap.

"Did Mom give you the good news about Popcorn?" I asked, taking a seat on the rocker-recliner.

"She did."

"I started to make *Paco* his middle name, but that would make his initials *PP*, and Popcorn and I thought that would be ridiculous." Mom looked down at Popcorn, who appeared content with whatever she called him as long as she called him for dinner and cuddles. "Besides, Kurt said *Popcorn* was an excellent name for the little darling's 'second act,' and I wholeheartedly agree."

"I wonder how the cat got out and wandered so far from home," Patty said.

"Kurt and I discussed that same thing." I pulled the lever of the recliner so I could put my feet up. "By the way, where have you been today?"

"I drove to a street fair in Brea Ridge. I'm sorry I didn't ask you or Mom to come with me, but I needed some alone time."

"We understand that, don't we?"

I wasn't sure whether the *we* Mom was referring to was she and I or her and Popcorn, but I nodded in agreement.

"I'm so nervous about the play," Patty continued. "Do you think the theater patrons will think I'm tacky for going ahead with the performance?"

"Of course, they won't," I said. "Everyone understands that the show must go on. I mean, that's the literal show business slogan, right?"

"And I won't mess up the part," Mom said. "You don't have to worry about that. I've practically got my lines down pat already."

"I know, Mom. I just don't want people to feel I'm being insensitive."

"If anyone was going to find it insensitive, I'd imagine it would be Imelda's family," I said. "But Kurt hasn't said one word against the play going forward as planned."

Patty's phone rang so loudly that even Popcorn raised his head and squinted at her indignantly.

"Sorry, Your Majesty." She answered the call. "Hi, Cassie... What?... Was anyone hurt?... I'll be right there."

By the time Patty had ended the call, I'd put down the footrest and stood. "Where are we going?"

"To the theater. Cassie and her dad were there—the staircase still doesn't suit him, although I think it looks fine—and a light fell and barely missed him."

"Is everybody okay?" Mom asked.

"Yes, he and Cassie are both fine, and they were the only people there. And Gerald was able to fix the light, but I'm still going over there. I need to check everything out for myself."

On the drive to the theater, I noticed Patty starting to bite her nails.

"Don't," I said. "Everything will be fine. Your teeth and your nails need you to keep your hands firmly in your lap."

"Easier said than done. What if someone is trying to sabotage the play?"

"Who would do that? Besides, didn't you say Cassie and Gerald were the only ones there? If they were trying to sabotage the play, they certainly wouldn't have called you to report the vandalism, would they?"

"I guess not. But they're not the only people who have keys to the theater," she said.

"Who else does?"

"The cleaning crew, Billy—because he and Gerald work on the sets together, you know."

"Okay, I confess. It was me. I'm sabotaging the play, but I wanted it to be a surprise."

"Dina, this is serious."

"I know." I reached over and squeezed her hand. "But I don't think anyone is sabotaging the play. I believe you're letting your nerves get the best of you." I supposed I was being insensitive. "You don't have to put this play on yet if you don't feel like it. If this is not something you're up to doing, use Imelda's death as a reason to delay it. If—"

"I *am* ready. I'm loving this job. It's given me something to look forward to every day for the first time since Gregory smashed my heart into a billion pieces. And I think I'm good at running the theater."

"I know you are."

She took an extended breath in through her nose and blew it out of her mouth. "I'll be fine." Another deep breath. "I can do this."

"Yes, you can." I knew my sister wasn't some fragile little flower. But she *was* delicate. Maybe less like a flower and more like a spider plant—still vulnerable but much sturdier.

Cassie and Gerald were waiting for us inside the theater. Gerald took Patty to show her where the light had fallen. I lagged behind to talk with Cassie.

"What does your dad think?" I whispered. "Does he think someone caused the light to fall?"

"No. We were the only ones here."

"Yeah, but someone could've loosened a screw or something, couldn't they?"

"I suppose that's possible, but Dad told me he believed it fell due to normal wear and tear." She patted my shoulder. "Don't look for trouble where there might not be any."

"Good advice but try telling my sister that."

Patty and Gerald returned.

"From now on, I want everything checked on a daily basis," Patty was saying. "I don't want to risk anything happening to the performers or crew members. Did you look for any other signs of…of damage?"

"I did." He nodded toward his daughter. "Cassie can attest to the fact that I went over every light, every microphone, *everything* twice."

Cassie gave a solemn nod.

"Everything looked fine," Gerald continued. "And from now on, I'll personally check the rigging every day before practice and before each performance when the play opens to the public."

Patty breathed a sigh of relief. "Thank you."

"Don't thank me. My daughter spends more time on that stage than anybody. It's her I'm looking out for."

Chapter Eleven

The shop was typically quiet first thing on a Monday morning, and today was no exception. I took out my phone to check my social media account. I had one new message. Holding my breath, I clicked the message tab.

Yes! It's from her!

The message was from the only *Usual Suspects* member we'd been able to reach out to yesterday evening. Her name was Agnes Harper Rollins, and she wrote:

I'm terribly sorry to learn of Imelda's passing. She was a dear friend to me in New York in the early '80s.

Since Agnes was still online, I immediately responded: *Kurt, Imelda's grandson, and I are trying to learn more about Imelda's life in New York. Would you be able to video chat with the two of us later today or tomorrow?*

Agnes wrote back that she'd be happy to video chat with us today over lunch. I told her that would be great.

As I waited for Kurt to answer his phone, I decided that even if he couldn't make it, I still wanted to talk with Agnes while I had the chance. I was eager to hear what she had to say.

"Good morning." Kurt sounded drowsy.

"I'm sorry. Did I wake you?"

"No. I was up too late last night and am feeling it today, that's all."

"I have some good news." I told him about the message from Agnes and about our upcoming video chat. "Will you be able to make it?"

"Absolutely. I wouldn't miss it." He paused. "I asked both Mom and Dad about Gran ever talking to them about her life in New York. He said she'd speak about the movie premieres and other events she attended once in a while, but that she refused to talk about her old life there. She said that was the past and that she preferred to live in the present."

"That makes sense."

"Yeah. Whether Randolph Gianetti was murdered or committed suicide, that was a painful time in her life. I can understand why she'd want to put it behind her."

"And yet she really hadn't," I said softly. "She wanted to know—or prove—the truth."

"She did. That's why I agree that it's imperative that we speak with Agnes Rollins. I'll see you a little before noon. Did your mom send lunch?"

I laughed. "I'm afraid not."

"I'll bring something then."

The mail carrier came in with a box I was expecting and placed it on the counter. "I remember where I saw the cat from your flyers. It used to sit in the window at Imelda Marshall's house."

"You're right. Imelda's grandson, Kurt, recognized the cat, said neither he nor his parents could keep it, and allowed my mom to adopt it."

"I'm so glad. Also, considering the circumstances, I'm relieved the cat got out of the house before Ms. Marshall died. Animals can be traumatized by seeing their owners hurt." She tsked. "You might want to tell your mom that Ms. Marshall had a strong citrus air freshener near the front and back doors to keep the cat from going near them. I know because she bought those things in bulk from a pet supply company, and one day, I flat out asked her what she did with them. As far as I knew, she only had the one cat, and I didn't think it would be that smelly."

"Kurt said the cat had a tendency to wander and that his grandmother kept a vigilant watch on him."

"She sure did. I used to think it was mean of her not to ever let the little guy outside but given that it got itself lost the first chance it had makes me think the air fresheners were a good idea." She smiled. "It's a sunny start to the week. Hope you get out of here in time to enjoy it today."

"Thanks. Have a good one!"

Opening the box of *The Wizard of Oz* playing cards, I considered what Liza had said. If there were deterrents in place to keep the cat away from both doors, how did he get out? I couldn't imagine Imelda would have left a window open. For one thing, it wasn't that warm out. But, most importantly, she wouldn't risk the cat escaping after taking precautions on the doors.

By the time I'd unpacked the box and stocked the playing cards with the rest of The Wizard of Oz merchandise, Cassie had arrived.

"Hey, there! How was class?"

She groaned. "Awful. I don't know why I have to take so many classes that have nothing to do with my major."

"And what's your major again?"

"I haven't decided yet."

I grinned. "And that answers your question."

"Ha ha." She picked up a deck of the cards. "These are cool. I'd like a deck."

"Take one."

She removed her wallet from her purse.

"Put that away," I said. "Consider it a bonus. I'm about to ask you to watch the shop for a few minutes while Kurt and I video chat with a woman who knew Imelda when she lived in New York."

"You and Kurt, huh?" She took the cards and opened them so she could look at each one. "The two of you are getting awfully friendly."

"He's a nice guy."

Glancing up from her cards, she said, "Not hard on the eyes either."

"I hadn't noticed."

She laughed. "Liar."

Kurt came into the shop then, saving me from a response but before the blush in my cheeks had subsided. "Hi. I know I'm early, but I brought food."

"Great," I said.

"You're flushed. Is everything all right?"

"Everything is fine. I've just been stocking some shelves." Jerking my chin in the direction of the bags he carried, I asked, "What have you got there?"

"Well, I was guessing Cassie would be here, so I brought enough steak biscuits, potato salad, and brownies for all of us."

"Gee, thanks!" Cassie put her cards back into the box and placed the box in her purse. "I didn't have time to eat breakfast this morning, and I'm more than ready to eat."

Kurt unpacked the food, and we helped ourselves. He and I took ours to my office, so we'd be ready for the video chat at noon.

"I hate to admit it, but I'm kinda nervous about this call." He unfolded a napkin and placed it on his lap.

"Don't be." I pulled my chair to the front of the desk so Kurt and I would be on the same side when we chatted with Agnes. "She seemed really nice, and I believe your grandmother meant a lot to her—at least, when they were living in New York."

"Yeah, I don't know that Gran kept in touch with too many people from her past. That's bound to alienate some of her former friends."

I shook my head. "People understand. How many times have you left a conference or a job or something and promised to keep in touch with someone—fully intending to do so—and life simply got in the way? It happens. Everybody knows that."

"Still—"

He was interrupted by the chime of the computer alerting us that Agnes was calling.

"Here goes." I answered the call. "Hi, Agnes. It's a pleasure to meet you. I'm Dina, and this is Kurt, Imelda's grandson."

"Nice to meet you both." Agnes's face softened as she gazed at Kurt. "Aren't you handsome? You were her pride and joy, you know."

"I..." He gulped. "Thank you."

"You're ever so welcome."

"How did you and Gran meet?"

"We lived in the same apartment complex. I was a dancer, and Imelda was searching for her big break in the acting world. Between auditions, she did secretarial work to keep from mooching off her parents all the time." Agnes smiled. "She'd moved out on her own to assert her independence, you know. Her parents wanted to marry her off to somebody with money. I'd have taken that option if I'd had it. In fact, I eventually did marry a wealthy man but not before a hip injury ended my dancing career."

"I'm so sorry," I said.

"Eh, I had a good run. I don't think Imelda realized how tough it was for a young woman to stand on her own two feet back then. I grew up hard, so it was all the same to me."

"I never heard Gran say anything about having a bad relationship with her parents," Kurt said.

"Oh, she didn't, dear. She simply wanted to show them that she could be her own person—that she could step out of their shadow and shine."

"And did she?" I asked.

"To an extent. I mean, she never got her acting career off the ground, but she was happy when she met Ran."

"Ran?" Kurt asked.

"Randolph Gianetti," Agnes said. "I truly thought she only started dating the man in order to try to break into the movies, but she wasn't ever in any of Ran's films. Not even as an extra. She said that would spoil everything. She wanted Ran to know beyond the shadow of a doubt that she loved him for him, not for anything he could do to advance her career."

"Do you think he was as crazy for her as she seemed to be about him?" I asked.

"I do. For the most part, everything about those two was romantic and sweet."

"For the most part?" Kurt prompted.

"Yeah. I mean, it turned sour in a heartbeat. I suppose you know he died?"

I nodded. "We saw his death mentioned in a couple of movie magazines. The general consensus appeared to be that Mr. Gianetti killed himself, but I don't think Imelda believed that."

"She didn't," Agnes said. "None of us did. That's why we formed our group—the *Usual Suspects*—to try to prove he was murdered."

"Who do you think killed Mr. Gianetti?" Kurt asked.

"His former girlfriend," Agnes said. "He threw her over for Imelda. When the police wouldn't listen to us and

Norah was never arrested, we eventually convinced Imelda to leave New York for her own safety."

I gasped. "You thought Norah was going to try to kill Imelda?"

"We were sure of it."

Chapter Twelve

After talking with Agnes, Kurt and I had even more questions. As we finished eating our lunch, we wondered about Agnes's assertions and what we knew of Imelda's life prior to coming to live in Skillet Ridge.

"If Imelda left New York in fear for her life, why didn't she change her name?" I asked between bites of potato salad.

"I don't know. I do know she didn't marry Grandpa until she'd been in Skillet Ridge for at least two years, and she used her maiden name before that."

"Then I think Agnes must've been wrong about Imelda fleeing for her life. Don't you?"

Wiping his mouth on his napkin, Kurt answered, "I'm not sure. Keep in mind how different times were then—she didn't have to worry about popping up on someone's social media or white page search."

"That's true. And Skillet Ridge would have been a wonderful hiding place. Who from New York would have ever heard of such a tiny town in Southwest Virginia?"

"And although Gran had friends in Johnson City, Tennessee, I don't think she had any ties to Skillet Ridge. She always told us she chose to live here because it's so beautiful." He smiled sadly. "I hope that was the case."

"I'm sure it was." I placed a hand on his arm. "She had a wonderful life here. There's at least one thing Agnes said that I believe unequivocally—you were your grandmother's pride and joy."

"Thank you." He took a bite of brownie and mulled over the situation as he chewed. At last, he said, "I'm going to reach out to Reggie Flax again to see if he knew Agnes or Norah."

"That's a good idea. I'm going to call Barry—he's my friend in New York who acquired the *Casablanca* script for me—and ask him if he can find out if any of Randolph Gianetti's relatives are still living and might be willing to talk with us."

"Great. Could we meet up later and compare notes?" he asked.

"Sure. You can come back by here or come to my apartment—whichever works best for you."

"Okay. If I'm not able to get back here before your shop closes, I'll see you at your apartment this evening."

"All right."

After taking some teasing from Cassie about how Kurt and I made a cute couple, I went back into my office, texted Barry, and asked if he had a minute to chat. Knowing he was a true crime buff, I thought he might be interested in the chance to help Kurt and me with our inquiries about who killed Randolph Gianetti and who might've wanted to murder Imelda.

I was right—he called me immediately.

"Dina, how are you doing?"

"I'm fine, but I could really use your help." I explained to him about Imelda's connection to Randolph Gianetti and how her grandson, Kurt, and I thought maybe Barry could see if any of the original investigators of the director's death were still around.

"I can do that," he said. "I'll also talk with the person from whom I bought the script to see if they have any connections to the Gianetti family."

"Thanks, Barry. You're the best."

"Be careful. This isn't a play or a movie you're working on. Someone actually killed this lady, and they might still be hanging around."

"I know," I said. "I'm well aware this isn't make-believe."

"I'm glad. I can't lose my best customer, you know." He chuckled. "I'll give you a shout when I have anything to report."

I thanked him again and ended the call. Maybe I was being ridiculous. How could a murder that happened over forty years ago have anything to do with Imelda Marshall's death? Odds were that Imelda was killed by a random person while she was out looking for her cat. And Imelda could have been entirely mistaken in her belief that Randolph Gianetti was murdered. Maybe he had been struggling with problems no one knew about. Maybe Kurt and I were looking for answers where there simply were none to be found.

Still, before I left my office, I did a search for *Randolph Gianetti and Norah*. Several images came up. I clicked on one and zoomed in. Norah had been an attractive woman—model thin with gaunt cheeks and large brown eyes. I zoomed in more. Were those crazy eyes—the eyes of a killer? Who could tell?

From the images, I learned that Norah's last name had been Steele; but a search for Norah Steele didn't turn up anything after Randolph Gianetti's death. It was as if she faded away. Maybe she changed her name or married someone else.

I heard the chime over the front door, and Cassie greeted our customer. When the customer spoke, he sounded like Reggie Flax. I closed my laptop and hurried out of the office.

It *was* Mr. Flax.

"Hi, there! Good to see you again, Mr. Flax."

"Hello, Dina."

"I'm glad you came by again before leaving town. Have you spoken with your wife?"

"N-no. Why?" He frowned at me so hard, his bushy white eyebrows came together as if they were one long albino caterpillar.

"I just wondered if she was feeling better."

"She's fine. She knew I planned to stay in Skillet Ridge for a couple of days. If she was sicker, she'd call and I'd go home, all right?"

"It wasn't my intention to come across as accusatory, Mr. Flax," I said. "I simply think it's too bad she couldn't accompany you on this trip. Maybe the two of you can return when Mrs. Flax is feeling better."

He relaxed, allowing the caterpillar to become two separate entities again. "Oh, sure. That would be nice. I believe she'd love this place."

I wasn't sure if he was talking about Lights, Camera, Action! or Skillet Ridge in general, so I simply smiled and nodded. "Mr. Flax, I spoke with a woman named Agnes Harper Rollins today."

He stiffened, his smile freezing in place.

"She was apparently part of Imelda's friend group when she was living in New York," I continued. "Did you know Agnes?"

"I knew her. She always had a flair for the dramatic. I wouldn't put too much stock in anything she said if I were you."

"Well, she did have a crazy story about how Imelda and some of their friends—including Agnes—believed that a woman named Norah Steele murdered Mr. Gianetti and wanted to kill Imelda too. She said that's why Imelda left New York."

"It was my understanding that Imelda left because she needed something new after Randolph's death...to go somewhere she'd never been in order to shake off the sadness."

"You were in love with Imelda, weren't you?" I asked softly.

He glanced around to make sure we weren't being overheard. We weren't. Cassie had her earphones in and was straightening up some shelves.

"Yes," he said simply.

"Then why didn't you come with her to Skillet Ridge?"

"I loved her, but she did not love me. Besides, I was still earning my college degree. I couldn't simply pull up stakes and sacrifice everything for Imelda, especially if she wasn't interested in the two of us creating a life together."

"I'm sorry."

Nodding, he said, "It was a long time ago. That heartache healed decades ago. In fact, I completely lost track of Imelda until social media became all the rage and she contacted some of us. She was still determined to see justice done on Randolph's behalf after all these years." He huffed. "Why couldn't she have simply let the past remain buried?"

"Do you feel like her dredging up the past is why she's dead now?" I asked.

He looked at his watch. "I'm sorry. I need to go."

Before I could consider Mr. Flax's strange behavior, a customer came in who was having a *Back to the Future-*themed party for her sister. She bought a movie poster, standees of both the main characters, some photo props, and a few tiny DeLorean keyrings for party favors. We brainstormed for a few minutes about what other party favors and refreshments she could serve in keeping with the theme. By the time she left, I was really wanting to attend that party myself.

I started when Cassie placed her hand on my shoulder.

She laughed. "Sorry. Time for you to come back to the future or the present or whatever."

"Right. I also need to order some more standees."

"Who'd have thought those things would be so popular?" she asked. "I mean, they're fun, but they're huge. Do people keep them standing in their rooms or put them away or what?"

"I have no idea."

"I'm getting ready to head out. I don't want to leave, though, if you think that Mr. Flax will come back in."

"Why's that?" I asked.

"I don't know. He just gives me a creepy vibe. I was only pretending to have my earphones in while you were talking with him. I wanted to be fully aware of what was going on."

"Thanks for that. He is kinda weird. He got so defensive when I asked about his wife."

"Right? Maybe he killed her or something."

My eyes widened.

"I'm kidding," she said quickly.

Neither of us was really convinced of that.

Chapter Thirteen

I was making nachos in the microwave when Kurt rang my doorbell.

"Hi," I said, opening the door. "Do you like nachos?"

"Is there anyone who *doesn't* like nachos?" He grinned. "I'm afraid I don't have anything new to report. Even though I called him several times, Reggie Flax didn't answer his phone."

"That's okay. He came into Lights, Camera, Action! this afternoon." I was telling Kurt about my conversation with Reggie when the microwave dinged.

Before removing the nachos from the microwave, I got each of us a plate. "What would you like to drink?"

"Whatever you have. I'm not picky."

I placed the nachos and plates on the table and poured each of us a glass of root beer. "We can have something more substantial later if—"

"No, this is fine. Thank you."

We sat at the table, and I finished telling him about Reggie's visit.

"That's so weird that he believes my grandmother is dead because she was looking into Randolph Gianetti's death. I haven't seen anything, other than the *Usual Suspects* notebook, that would suggest she was investigating a crime."

"Was there anything in there about who Imelda or any of the other members of the *Usual Suspects* believed killed Gianetti?" I asked.

He shook his head. "The only thing in that notebook was the list of names. I'm guessing that at some time or another, Gran decided to delve into the murder and then abandoned the notion as being pointless."

"That, or there's additional information hidden in your grandmother's home."

My phone buzzed.

It was Barry calling.

I wiped my hands on my napkin before answering the call. "Hi, Barry. I'm here with Kurt, Imelda's grandson, and I'm going to make this a video call so we can all discuss what you've found."

"Great. Nice to meet you, Kurt."

"Likewise," Kurt said.

I moved my chair next to Kurt's so Barry could see and hear us both clearly when I set my phone up in front of us. "Do I need to take notes?"

"I don't think so," Barry said. "But I do have some interesting information. I found someone who worked on the case—he was a rookie at the time. He took a look in the file and said that there were two witnesses who gave statements about Randolph Gianetti's death. They were Reginald Flax and Agnes Harper."

My jaw dropped. "Are you kidding?"

"No, why?"

I told Barry about our encounters with both Reggie and Agnes. "What did the witness statements say?"

"The detective said Mr. Flax reported that Mr. Gianetti had been despondent and had been talking about committing suicide. Agnes Harper said pretty much the same thing—Gianetti had been depressed and hadn't wanted to go on."

"Oh, my gosh." I raised my hand to my throat. "Is it possible one or both of them killed Gianetti? What if Agnes was really Gianetti's ex-girlfriend? If she killed him, Reggie might've backed up the suicide story because he was glad Gianetti was no longer standing between him and Imelda."

"But she's the one who brought up the ex-girlfriend in the first place," Kurt said. "Why would she do that if *she* was the ex-girlfriend?"

"Agnes also said that she didn't believe Randolph Gianetti committed suicide," I reminded him. "If that was true, why did she give a statement to the police at the time saying she did?"

Barry tapped his fingertips together. "The plot thickens."

"We should return to Gran's house to see if we can find any other information about Gianetti's death," Kurt said.

"In the meantime, I'll do some digging into Reginald Flax and Agnes Harper," Barry said.

"It's Agnes Harper Rollins now, if that helps," I said.

Barry reached for a pen and paper and wrote down Agnes's full name. "I'll let you know if I'm able to uncover anything."

"We'll do the same," Kurt said. "Thank you for your help."

"Glad to do it. I'm sorry for your loss, man."

"Do you think the two—" I struggled for the kindest word—"*incidents* could be connected?"

"I do." Barry opened his mouth as if he wanted to expound on his opinion, but he closed it again. I was guessing he didn't want to say anything that might be painful for Kurt to hear.

After we finished our nachos and I put our dishes in the dishwasher, Kurt and I headed to Imelda's place. We discussed everything we knew so far as we drove, but it wasn't much.

We knew that Reggie Flax had visited Imelda at the theater at least once—maybe twice. Why had he visited her? How long had he really been in town? And why hadn't he left after the memorial? Especially if he had a sick wife at home.

Agnes spoke about Imelda as if they'd been besties when they were living in New York. But had they been? Agnes knew a lot about Imelda, but she seemed a little envious of the fact that Imelda came from money while Agnes herself grew up impoverished. While it wasn't out of the question that Agnes was the woman Gianetti "threw over" for Imelda, Kurt and I didn't put a lot of credence in that theory because she was the one who'd brought up the possibility of the ex-girlfriend murdering Gianetti and said her name was Norah. Agnes *could* have been having a laugh at our expense—maybe her middle name was Norah or Norah Steele was her stage name—but it was doubtful.

And what about Phil? He hadn't liked Reggie. Did he know Reggie? That was a lead we needed to follow up on.

As Kurt drove closer to Imelda's house, I said, "Stop!"

He slammed on the brakes, causing the seatbelt to catch me as I was flung forward. "What's wrong?"

"I thought I saw a light in your grandmother's house."

He turned off his headlights and pulled into the driveway. We watched for a moment and saw the light moving again.

"It's a flashlight," Kurt said. "There's someone in there with a flashlight."

"I'm calling Detective Tilson." I took out my phone.

"Good. You stay in the car. I'm going inside."

"Kurt, you can't! We don't know who's in there and whether or not they're armed!"

"Whoever is in there might be the person who killed my grandmother. I'm not giving them a chance to get away."

As Kurt got out of the car, I called Detective Tilson and quickly explained that Kurt and I were at Imelda Marshall's house and that there was someone inside. "Kurt has gone in to make sure the prowler doesn't escape."

"Oh, fantastic." Her voice indicated it was anything but fantastic that Kurt had gone into the house. "I'll get officers to the home as quickly as possible." She ended the call.

I put down my phone and wondered what else I could do. I didn't want Kurt to have to face a criminal—or *criminals*—by himself. I didn't want to get killed either. I got out of the car, pushed the door closed as quietly as I could, and eased closer to the house.

The curtains were slightly open in the living room. I peered through the narrow space but couldn't see anything.

And then the lights came on, and I could see everything—everything being Kurt and Reggie Flax standing toe to toe. Reggie appeared to be frightened. Kurt was furious.

I hurried inside. "What's going on?"

"That's what I'd like to know," Kurt said.

Reggie looked at me, his eyes pleading. "You know I'd never hurt Imelda. I cared for her."

"Then what are you doing here snooping around her house in the dark?" I asked.

"I wanted to find whatever evidence Imelda had that convinced her that Randolph Gianetti was murdered."

"Did you murder Gianetti?" Kurt asked.

"No," Reggie said, "but I'm afraid my wife might've. If she did, it was an accident. She'd have never hurt anyone on purpose."

I heard sirens blaring, and they were getting closer. "Reggie, do you think your wife murdered Imelda?"

His face crumpled. "I'm sorry for all of this. I don't want to go to jail."

Detective Tilson's voice boomed over a loudspeaker. "Everyone in the house, come out the front door with your hands up. Be advised there are armed officers surrounding the house, and you'd be wise to follow my instructions."

We followed the detective's instructions. I could tell she was already put out with all of us. Kurt and I should have stayed in the car.

I was the first one out of the house, hands raised. "Sorry."

Detective Tilson rolled her eyes. "I'm not even surprised."

Mr. Flax came out next, followed by Kurt.

Nodding her head at the older man, Detective Tilson said, "I take it you're our prowler?"

"Yes, ma'am. I'm very sorry. Would it be possible for me to get off with a warning?" He grimaced. "I promise never to do it again."

"No, that won't be possible." The detective nodded at another officer who walked Mr. Flax toward a police cruiser. "As for you two, what you did—going into a house with an intruder inside—was pretty stupid. You had no idea what you might face when you opened that door."

"We know," Kurt said. "In Dina's defense, she didn't come inside until she saw that the prowler was Mr. Flax and that he wasn't armed."

I hadn't realized Mr. Flax wasn't armed, but it had become clear to me before I entered the home that Kurt had the situation under control, so I kept my mouth shut.

"Do you two know this man?" Detective Tilson asked.

"He was at my grandmother's memorial, and before that, he visited Gran at the theater," Kurt said.

"And he's been to my shop a couple of times," I said.

"All right." She turned to leave.

"Detective Tilson?"

She looked back at Kurt.

"Will you keep us posted? If you find anything that leads you to believe he killed Gran?"

Considering her words carefully, she said, "When we make an arrest in your grandmother's murder, you'll be the first to know, Mr. Marshall. In the meantime, leave the investigating to the professionals please."

As soon as the police cars were gone, Mary stepped out onto her porch and called, "Is everything okay over there?"

I could barely hear her over Skippy's barking. He was in Mary's backyard racing back and forth behind a chain-link fence.

"Yes, Mary, it's fine," Kurt called. "There was...um...an old friend of my grandmother's who broke into her house to look for something he believed he'd left there."

Flattening her mouth into a thin line, she said, "I know you're just trying not to scare me. If that man had really been a friend of your grandmother's, he'd have used the spare key she kept in the birdhouse instead of breaking in."

"Have you seen an older, white-haired man coming around Imelda's house lately?" I asked.

"I'm not sure," she said. "I try to keep to myself. But with everything that's been happening around here, I'm about ready to put my own house up for sale and leave. Who'd have ever thought Skillet Ridge could be so dangerous?"

Kurt and I wished her goodnight and then went inside to see if we could figure out what Reggie had been searching for.

Chapter Fourteen

Reggie had been neat in his search. Nothing appeared to have been disturbed. The Robert Redford photo was slightly crooked, so I took it off the wall and turned it over. There was nothing on the back. I sat down on the sofa and removed the back from the frame. The photograph was the only thing in the frame. I replaced the back and put the photo back on the wall.

Sighing as I turned to look at Kurt, who was going through the desk, I asked, "Anything?"

"Nothing we haven't seen before."

"Maybe we're looking in the wrong place. Your grandmother was a smart woman. She'd know that if anyone broke into her house looking for something she was hiding about Randolph Gianetti, they'd assume it was in this room. Where else did she spend the most time?"

"Well, she always read the newspaper at the kitchen table," he said. "I feel as if we've exhausted our search here. What would it hurt to poke around in the kitchen?"

I followed him into Imelda's bright, tidy kitchen. "Where would you like me to look?"

"I'll take the cabinets, and you take the drawers?"

"Works for me." In addition to searching the drawers, I removed them and held them up over my head to make sure there wasn't anything taped to the bottoms. My years of watching detective shows hadn't been wasted.

It was in the drawer closest to the floor and farthest from the sink that I finally found something interesting. Beneath a magazine, there was a photograph that had been torn out of a movie magazine. With the photo, there was a magnifying glass.

"Kurt, what do you make of this?" I took the photo and the magnifying glass from the drawer. "I believe Imelda was studying this photo."

He joined me at the kitchen table where I placed the photo and examined it through the magnifying glass myself.

"I don't see anything unusual about it." I handed him the magnifying glass.

"Would you go get us one of those magazines containing images of Randolph Gianetti? I think this is the woman he dated before Gran."

I retrieved a stack of the magazines and brought them back to the kitchen. I quickly thumbed through them while Kurt scanned the photo I'd found in the drawer. At last, I came to a photo of a woman with Randolph Gianetti. The picture appeared to have been taken on the same evening as the one Imelda had been studying. At least, in this photo—taken at a charity event—the woman was wearing the same dress as she was in Imelda's magazine clipping.

"Isn't this the woman whose image your grandmother was studying?" I pushed the magazine closer to Kurt.

He glanced between the two photos, and then looked at the one still in the magazine through the magnifying glass. "It is." He read the name in the caption. "*Randolph Gianetti and Norah Steele.*"

"So, this is Norah." I gave both photographs more careful consideration. "I wonder why Imelda was examining this photo?"

"I don't have a clue. Maybe we can find something else that will be more telling."

Kurt and I searched the kitchen and the living room for another hour before we decided to call it a night.

"You made a smart call suggesting Gran wouldn't hide anything here in her house. I'll check her safe deposit box at the bank tomorrow," he said.

"And I'll send Agnes another message. In fact, I'll do it now, since what she told us and what she told the police all those years ago don't mesh up."

I opened my social media account and messaged Agnes: *Hi, Agnes. Kurt and I really enjoyed speaking with you earlier today, and we thank you for your time. We recently learned that you told police at the time of Randolph Gianetti's death that he'd been depressed and hadn't wanted to go on living. We'd like to talk with you about that if you have some time within the next day or so.*

Agnes was online and immediately fired back: *Of course, that's what I told the police. I wasn't about to say anything that would have put myself in the killer's crosshairs. I have nothing further to say on the matter. I'm sorry for your loss, but please don't bother me anymore.*

"Well, I guess that's that," I said.

"I suppose it is. Hopefully, I can find something helpful in the safe deposit box."

"And there's always the possibility Barry will find out more. He's a true crime junkie. He'll tear into the investigation of Randolph Gianetti's death like a dog with a porterhouse steak."

Kurt gave me a sad smile. "Gran would've liked Barry."

First thing Tuesday morning, Detective Tilson came by Lights, Camera, Action! to give me an update about Reggie Flax.

"I've already spoken with the Marshall family, but I also wanted to keep you apprised of what's happening," Detective Tilson said. "Reginald Flax was charged with breaking and entering, and he was released on bond. The Marshall family didn't feel the need to obtain a restraining order against Mr. Flax; but since you said he'd been here to your shop more than once, I wanted to alert you about Mr. Flax's release and see if you require a restraining order."

"I don't think that's necessary," I said, "but thank you for the information."

"You're welcome. Please let me know if Mr. Flax makes contact with you again or if you discover anything missing from Ms. Marshall's residence the next time you're there." She paused. "Look, Dina, I know you and Kurt Marshall are conducting your own investigation. And while I'd prefer you didn't, I would appreciate being kept informed if you discover anything that might be relevant to Ms. Marshall's death."

"Of course. We're mainly attempting to learn about events of Imelda's life that came to light after her death. For instance, we learned that she was engaged to the director, Randolph Gianetti, at the time of his death. The death was suspicious. It was eventually ruled a suicide, but some people continue to assert that he was murdered."

"I'll look into it." She took out her notebook, quickly scribbled something, and tucked the notebook back into her pocket. "I'm skeptical a decades-old suspicious death would factor into the murder of Imelda Marshall, but I'll see if I can uncover any links."

During the late morning lull, I was looking at an online auction site at some movie memorabilia when Barry texted me to say he had more information about how Randolph Gianetti died.

I immediately initiated a video chat. "What have you found?"

"Good morning!" He smiled into the camera. "I'm doing great, thanks. And how are you?"

"Impatient."

"As always." He chuckled. "You still should mind your manners though."

Rolling my eyes, I said, "Sorry. Good morning, Barry."

"Much better. Thank you."

"I do apologize for being rude. Last night was crazy, and I was truly hoping we could find something soon that might help put us on the right track." I told Barry about Kurt and me finding Reggie Flax at Imelda's house last night when we returned to look for more evidence into Randolph Gianetti's death. "And Detective Tilson has already been by here this morning to tell me Mr. Flax has been released on bond and to see if I wanted a restraining order against him."

"What did you say?" Barry asked.

"I said I didn't feel it was necessary."

"Because you don't believe Mr. Flax was responsible for killing Imelda or because you still want to have access to the man to find out if he *did* murder her?"

Expelling a breath, I said, "I don't know. Both, maybe? He told Kurt and me last night that he didn't kill Rudolph Gianetti but that he's afraid his wife might have."

"First of all, what? Why would he marry someone he suspected of murder?"

"I thought that same thing."

"And second, if she killed Gianetti, then she's definitely the one who killed Imelda," he continued.

"What makes you so sure?"

"The person who murdered Randolph Gianetti was attempting to harm Imelda Marshall. The brake lines had been disconnected on her car—a little Porsche—and that was the vehicle Gianetti was driving when he slammed into a tree head on. He was killed on impact."

A chill sliced through me. "Imelda was meant to have that accident."

"Exactly."

"Wasn't her statement in the file? Surely, the police had spoken with her about it."

He shook his head. "No mention of Imelda Marshall was made anywhere in the record of Randolph Gianetti's death."

"That's so weird. Why would they talk with Reggie Flax and Agnes Harper but not the victim's fiancée—the owner of the car he'd been driving?"

"I'm guessing Imelda's parents kept her out of it. They were apparently pretty influential in and around the city."

"Were they government officials or something?" I asked.

"All I know is that they had some clout."

"Oh." A thought occurred to me. "No one thinks *Imelda* killed Randolph, do they?"

Shrugging, Barry said, "Anything is possible. Don't rule out that she didn't."

"Barry!"

"Do you want the truth or whatever will make you and Kurt Marshall feel better?" he asked.

"I want the truth."

"Then be prepared to accept it, whatever it is. I'll keep searching."

"Me too," I said softly. "I'll keep you posted on my findings."

"I'll do the same."

After ending the chat, I sat staring into space for several minutes. Was what Barry said possible? Could Imelda have tampered with the brakes herself and sent Randolph off to be in an accident? Maybe she believed he was cheating on her, or she decided she didn't love him enough to marry him after all. But I couldn't imagine her disconnecting the brake lines on her own car in the hope that Randolph would drive it and wreck. There were far easier ways to get out of a relationship.

Still, were her parents powerful enough to keep Imelda from even being questioned about her fiancé's death? To keep the police from doing a proper investigation at all? To keep justice from being served?

Was that why Imelda had been killed? Had someone avenged Randolph Gianetti's death all these years later?

What was I going to say to Kurt?

Chapter Fifteen

I was still wondering how I could ask Kurt just how influential his great-grandparents had been since they'd kept their daughter out of Randolph Gianetti's police report when Patty called.

"Have you got a minute?" she asked.

"Yes. You sound serious."

"This could be serious. Can anyone else hear me?"

"No. I'm in my office alone, and I don't have you on speaker anyway. What's going on?"

"Last night after play practice, I found a key on the floor. The key had a blue tag on it. I picked it up and went around to everyone who was still at the theater to ask if they'd lost it. I didn't want anyone to arrive home and realize they couldn't get into their home."

"Okay," I said. "So, whose key was it?"

"Imelda's."

Now Patty had my full attention.

"Alfred is the one who told me it was hers," Patty continued, "and he said he was the one who'd lost it. He told me it must've fallen through a hole in his pants pocket."

"What was he doing with it?"

"According to Alfred, Imelda had given it to him a few weeks ago when she went out of town and asked him to feed her cat. He acted as if he'd forgotten he even had it and mumbled something about getting it back to her family before he dropped it back into his pocket...presumably the one without the hole."

"If he'd forgotten about even having it, what was he doing carrying it around in his pocket?" I tapped my pen on the desk. "That sounds sketchy to me."

"It does to me too," she said. "That's why I called to get your opinion. Even if Imelda did give him the key for whatever reason, don't you find it odd that he'd be carrying it around after her death?"

Sighing, I tried to give Alfred the benefit of the doubt. "I don't know. If Imelda traveled often and Alfred was accustomed to caring for the cat when she was gone, or if they were dating, it might've been convenient for Imelda and Alfred to have keys to each other's homes."

"That's true. Their having keys to each other's places wouldn't be at all unusual. I mean, neighbors often do that too, right?" She paused. "But Alfred *was* the one who drove Imelda home that night."

"Right, but Mary, Imelda's neighbor, never mentioned anything about hearing a car drive off—at least, not to me. And I believe it was after Alfred had been gone for a little while that Mary found Imelda."

"We don't know how long she'd been lying out there, though." She groaned. "I don't want to believe Alfred would hurt Imelda either. He seems as sweet as can be, and he and Imelda appeared to have cared for each other."

"Until Phil butted in," I muttered. "That's what you said, right?"

"I don't know, Dina. Am I making a mountain out of a mole hill?"

"Not at all. We don't know who killed Imelda. And you're working with these people every evening. We need to be wary of everybody until we know who did murder her." I took a deep breath. "Speaking of which—"

"What? Wait, no. Don't tell me. I don't know whether or not I can take any more bad news today."

"It isn't exactly bad news," I said.

"All right. Tell me then."

"Barry learned from the police report that Randolph Gianetti died in a car accident because someone had tampered with the brakes."

"But didn't you tell me his death was ruled a suicide?"

"Yeah, I did. Which doesn't make sense. If he wanted to kill himself, why would he tamper with the brakes? He'd just drive into the tree."

"Hmm. Maybe he tampered with the brakes because he was afraid that he'd back out?" She was playing devil's advocate—much like the police must have done.

"Okay. Let's say he did. He didn't want to have the option to change his mind at the last minute. But get this—the car belonged to Imelda."

"Oooh, so the accident was supposed to have happened to her."

"Or she knew Randolph would be driving her car, and she's the one who tampered with the brakes." I let that statement hang in the air for a second before adding, "And her parents kept her name out of the police report entirely."

"No." She clucked her tongue. "I don't think so. I can't imagine Imelda under the hood of a car or removing a tire to get to the brake lines or whatever it was she would have had to do."

"You can't imagine her doing it since you've known her. You don't know anything about what she was like before she came here to Skillet Ridge. Not even her family knows much about her past."

"I'm still not buying it," Patty said. "I don't care how powerful her parents were, if the police had believed or had enough evidence to prove Imelda was guilty of Randolph Gianetti's death, they'd have prosecuted her."

"I don't know. Like you, I initially thought Imelda was likely the intended victim, but the fact that there was no mention of her at all in the police report even though the man was driving her car seems awfully dodgy to me. How do I bring this up to Kurt?"

"You don't! Dina, you don't *know* anything about what happened to Randolph Gianetti. All we truly know is this—a woman who was loved by her family is dead, and you're about to let your morbid curiosity sabotage your chance at a relationship with Kurt."

"I'm more interested in the truth than in a relationship with Imelda Marshall's grandson." I wasn't as sure of that fact as I hoped I sounded. "Sure, I'm attracted to Kurt, but I don't even really know him yet. And my sister could be working with a murderer. We have to find out who killed Imelda and why."

"You worry about you, and let me worry about me," she said. "Don't say something insensitive to Kurt. Think about how you'd feel if we found out that Mom had some deep, dark secret from her past."

I laughed.

"I'm serious. Everybody has a past."

"Not Mom," I said.

"Even Mom. Now, are you coming to the theater this evening?"

"Yes. I'll see you there."

I closed the shop a little early and drove to nearby Brea Ridge to visit the library. Although I'd looked through all the magazines Kurt and I had found at Imelda's house, I knew there were issues—as well as other magazines—that might have additional information about Randolph, his old girlfriend, his death, and possibly even Imelda.

Inside the hushed library, I approached the reference desk and requested access to specific movie magazine articles from the time period surrounding Randolph's short period of fame and his demise. The librarian, a kindly elderly woman, assisted me in locating the relevant microfilm reels.

I carefully threaded the film onto the microfilm reader and began scrolling through the faded pages of history. I scanned through article after article, searching for any mention of Randolph Gianetti, Norah Steele, or Imelda. It dawned on me that I didn't even know Imelda's maiden name.

After what felt like an eternity, my eyes widened as I stumbled upon a photograph of Imelda, Randolph Gianetti, and a middle-aged couple. The headline read,

New Up and Coming Director Randolph Gianetti Steps Out with Cappitani Family.

Okay. So, Imelda's maiden name was Cappitani. I read the provocative article, becoming more and more stunned by what I was learning:

In a surprising turn of events, acclaimed director Randolph Gianetti was seen in the company of the mysterious Cappitani family at a glamorous industry event held last night. The presence of the Cappitanis, known for their shadowy connections and rumored ties to organized crime, has left tongues wagging and speculation running rampant in Hollywood circles.

Imelda Cappitani, the striking beauty who has caught Gianetti's eye, was seen radiating charm and elegance as she mingled effortlessly with the who's who of the film industry. While Gianetti is still a rising star in the directing realm, the Cappitani name carries weight and influence that extends far beyond the silver screen.

As Randolph Gianetti and Imelda Cappitani stepped into the spotlight, the pair exuded an undeniable chemistry that captivated onlookers. Witnesses describe their interaction as intense and magnetic, leaving little doubt that their connection extends beyond mere professional collaboration.

However, with Gianetti's star on the rise and the Cappitani family's notorious reputation preceding them, questions linger about the nature of their association. Is this a case of a talented director finding inspiration in the arms of a captivating woman, or is there more to their relationship than meets the eye?

While some speculate that Gianetti's involvement with the Cappitani family may lead to unprecedented opportunities in the industry, others fear that his association with such powerful and potentially dangerous figures could spell trouble in the long run. Hollywood has witnessed its fair share of love affairs gone wrong and entanglements that have led to unforeseen consequences, and the Gianetti-Cappitani alliance seems poised to join the ranks of those tales.

Only time will tell how this intriguing love story unfolds, and whether it will be marked by success, scandal, or something far more sinister. As the cameras continue to roll and the drama unfolds both on and off the screen, one thing is certain—when Randolph Gianetti steps out with the Cappitani family, the spotlight shines brighter, and the stakes become higher.

I gulped. No wonder Imelda's name wasn't mentioned in that police report.

Chapter Sixteen

I was still shaken up by the news that Imelda's family was involved in organized crime as I drove to the theater. That was a lot to take in. Had Imelda herself ever been involved in the family business? Had her son? Had Kurt? *Was* Kurt?

What should I do with this new information? If Imelda's family had wanted Randolph Gianetti out of the way, then any one of their hired muscle could have tampered with the brakes on Imelda's car. But would her family have taken such a risk? Certainly not without Imelda's knowledge. Otherwise, how could they be sure she wouldn't be the person driving the car when the brakes failed?

Or maybe I was jumping to the wrong conclusions. Maybe the crime family had nothing to do with Randolph Gianetti's death. Maybe it was as Patty had suggested—he'd sabotaged the car himself because he was afraid of backing out of the accident. Or to ensure that the wreck did indeed appear to be an accident. Furthermore, it was entirely possible that Randolph had never intended to kill himself...that he'd caused the accident as a publicity stunt, but it backfired on him. That could happen, right?

Not likely.

I'd printed out the article and stuffed it in my tote. I made a mental note to check the name of the writer and see if I could get in touch with him or her. Perhaps the journalist could answer some of my questions.

I stopped at a convenience store and got a soda and a bag of chips before going on to the theater. When I got there, Mom fussed at me for my crummy dinner choice; and I tried to explain that I hadn't had time to do better. She insisted I stop by her house after play practice for something more substantial. Patty called to her from up on stage—to my relief—and she went to rehearse her scene.

I sat down in the front row, unzipped my bag, and dropped my car keys inside before opening the chips.

Phil came and took a seat beside me. "Your mom is doing really well with the part."

"That's kind of you to say. I know Imelda's death hit you and everyone else here really hard."

"It did." He nodded. "But she would have wanted the show to go on without her, and she'd have been pleased that Anna Marie was able to step into the role."

"Thank you." Wondering if he'd told Mom that, I propped my open chip bag into the top of my tote so it didn't spill while I was opening my soda. I took a drink and recapped the bottle before removing the chips.

When I pulled the chips out of the tote, the article I'd printed out at the library got hung on the bottom of the bag and fluttered to the floor in front of me. Before I could retrieve it, Phil leaned down and picked it up.

He did a doubletake. "Where did you get this?"

"May I please have that back?"

Phil shoved the paper toward me, and I quickly folded it in half to hide the article's content before putting it back in my bag. Yes, I was aware it was a bit like closing the barn door after the horse had already gotten out and seen the incriminating article, but the rest of the stable was still in the dark.

Glaring at me, he said, "You should be careful about kicking hornets' nests. Not only might you get stung, but everyone around you could suffer too."

I opened my mouth to speak, but he turned and stalked off. I took another drink of my soda to soothe my suddenly parched throat.

After play practice, I went to Mom's house. Over sandwiches and milk, I showed Mom and Patty the article about Imelda and Randolph Gianetti.

"That's intriguing," Mom said. "Poor Imelda and Randolph, young lovers with an ill-fated romance. Maybe Randolph knew too much about the Cappitanis. Or maybe he saw something he was never meant to see, and some capo whacked him. Imelda was left heartbroken. She turned her back on her family and fled to Skillet Ridge, Virginia, the only place she felt she could truly escape and live outside her family's looming shadow."

Patty and I exchanged glances, hoping she was done. She was not.

"But, alas," Mom continued, "the Cappitanis found Imelda and forced her to marry the very capo who'd taken her beloved Randolph's life. She went through with the marriage, but she refused to leave charming Skillet Ridge, and eventually, she and the capo fell in love. You see, he'd always loved her from afar—that's why he volunteered to whack Randolph."

"Mom, do you even know what a capo is?" I asked.

"It's a guy who whacks people—everybody knows that. It's common knowledge in crime circles. Want somebody whacked? Call a capo."

"Did Imelda *know* the capo they forced her to marry was the one who'd killed Randolph?" Patty asked.

I gave my sister an open-mouthed stare. "Must you encourage her?"

"Why not?" Patty shrugged. "This is a good story."

"It isn't merely a story. Someone really did cause Randolph Gianetti's accident. I don't know if it was her family or—"

"Oooh!" Mom interrupted. "It could have been a rival crime family trying to take out Imelda to settle a score."

"Okay, yeah, that's possible," I agreed. "But it could've been Norah Steele. Or even Imelda herself."

"But what bearing does any of that have on Imelda's death?" Patty asked. "Randolph Gianetti died so long ago. How could anything involving him or his death have caused Imelda's murder after all this time? Her parents are dead. What? Are you thinking her son is still in the family business and that someone killed Imelda to send him a message?"

"I don't know." I put my head in my hands. "Maybe Phil was right. He warned me about kicking hornets' nests."

"He what?" Patty asked.

I raised my head, thinking maybe she hadn't understood my muffled words, and told her and Mom how Phil had sat beside me, saw the article, issued his dire warning, and then left. "I didn't see him again—other than onstage—for the rest of the evening. Oh, by the way, Mom, he bragged on your wonderful performance and said Imelda would have been pleased with how well you've taken on the role."

"Oh, that's so sweet." Mom beamed.

"Wait. Let's go back to Phil warning you not to kick hornets' nests," Patty said. "That seems pretty ominous, if you ask me. Do you think it's possible he's involved in the Cappitani family business? Or the rival family's business?"

"I don't know." I frowned. "You've known him longer than Mom or I have. What do you know about him?"

"Not much. He simply showed up and auditioned for the part of the telephone repairman." Patty sighed and pinched the bridge of her nose. "Dina, I'm so sorry for what I said earlier today."

"What did you say?" Mom asked.

"I told Dina not to sabotage a relationship with Kurt because of my suspicions. I mean, I'm a good one to talk, right? Everyone thought Richard was such a catch and that I was lucky to have landed him and look how *that* turned out."

"That doesn't mean Kurt is a Richard," Mom said. "I stand by what Patty told you earlier—don't ruin a possible relationship with Kurt due to rampant speculation. For all we know, Imelda was killed by some random psycho who just happened to be passing by that night."

Even though I was ninety-five percent certain that's *not* what happened, I said, "I know."

Mom's voice took on a more stern and serious tone. "No, you *don't* know. That's the whole point. Don't you dare add to that family's grief by dredging up Imelda's past when it could have absolutely no bearing on her death whatsoever. And if it *is* relevant, then let Detective Tilson discover that fact. She's good at her job. She doesn't need your help."

With that, Mom got up, said she was tired, and went to bed.

Patty and I looked at each other.

"What just happened?" she asked.

"I have no idea."

Chapter Seventeen

On Wednesday morning, I was pleasantly surprised when Patty strolled into my shop. A customer was buying a *Cocoon* T-shirt for her dad.

"I'm so happy I called you," she said. "This has always been one of Dad's favorite movies. He saw it in the theater with his grandfather when the movie first came out. It was a wonderful memory for him, and I know he'll love this shirt."

"I'm glad. Any time you need a particular item, please don't hesitate to let me know. If I can't find it, I probably know someone who can." I folded the shirt and placed it in a Lights, Camera, Action! bag. "Thank you again for coming in!"

"You're welcome. You can count on my coming back." With a smile at me and a nod at Patty, the woman took her purchase and left the shop.

As soon as the lady had gotten in her car, Patty asked, "You have merchandise from a movie that was released more than three decades ago?"

"Of course. A lot of my merchandise is for films even older than that one. I mean, I have stuff for new releases too, but people are nostalgic about their favorite movies." I smiled. "There was actually a bit of serendipity with her purchase. She called and asked if I had any *Cocoon* merchandise, and I happened to have bought a lot of vintage movie and TV t-shirts that contained a few *Cocoon* shirts. Luckily, there was one in her dad's size."

"That's pretty cool."

"Thanks. What brings you by?"

She shrugged slightly as if it was no big deal. Knowing Patty, that meant it was definitely a big deal. "Last night was crazy, don't you think?"

"What do you mean?" I asked.

"Mom. The way she got weird on us and went to bed when we started talking about asking Kurt's family about Imelda's past. Wonder why Mom would get all peculiar about that?"

"I have no idea. But, upon further reflection, I did decide that she was probably right in that I shouldn't be discussing Imelda's family and their organized crime associates with Kurt or anyone else in her family." I came around the counter to tidy a stack of *Star Wars* trading cards. "I scanned the article this morning and sent it to Barry. Maybe he can find something helpful. Besides, after giving it some consideration, I find it pretty unlikely that anyone involved in organized crime would be living in Skillet Ridge, Virginia."

"Imelda was living here," Patty was quick to point out.

"True, but we don't think she was actually involved in the family business, do we?"

"I don't know." She sighed. "Rather than becoming clearer, the mystery surrounding Imelda's death is getting murkier all the time."

"That's true. But you can't let Imelda's murder weigh you down. Rather than getting caught up in the investigation, focus on making the play the best it can possibly be and dedicating it to her memory."

"Like you're doing?"

Inclining my head, I said, "*Touche.* But my circumstances are different."

"Yeah, yours involve a handsome man who may or may not be a mobster."

"Kurt is not a mobster. I'm ninety-eight percent sure of that."

"Mmm…okay. Well, those are good statistics provided that two percent of doubt doesn't come back to bite you."

Desperate for Patty to get off the subject of Kurt, I asked, "So, what deep dark secret do you think Mom might be harboring?"

"Well, the first thing that sprang to mind was a secret child. Do you think we might have an older sibling out there somewhere? One that was born to Mom when she was young, before she met Dad?"

"No! Mom could've never kept something like that quiet. And as soon as the internet became a thing, she'd have been looking for her abandoned child." I straightened the *Deadpool* trading cards. "Knowing Mom, she only wanted us to think she has a deep, dark secret. More likely, it's nothing more than a shallow, dim, conundrum."

"You're probably right."

I stepped over and put my arm around her shoulders. "Of course, I'm right. I'm the smart one."

She gave me a playful shove. "Will you be at play practice tonight?"

"I'll be there."

Turning to leave, she saw Alfred getting ready to come inside and waited. "Hi, Alfred."

"Welcome to Lights, Camera, Action," I told him.

"Thank you." The older man was wearing a bucket hat, which he removed when he stepped into the shop. "I realized I'd never taken the opportunity to check out your store, Dina, and when I noticed Patty's car here, I decided to pop in, say hello, and see what sort of merchandise you have."

"I'm glad you did," I said.

He walked in front of the register, glanced down one of the aisles, and said, "Before I get lost in my browsing, I wondered if I might ask a brazen question. I won't be offended in the slightest if you tell me no and that you'd prefer not to answer my inquiry."

Shooting a nervous glance in Patty's direction, I told Alfred to ask away.

"I'd like to know what was on that paper Phil saw last night at the theater," he said. "I saw you drop it, he picked it up, and then he acted like a bear with a sore paw the rest of the night. I asked him about it, and he told me to mind my own business."

Again, I looked at Patty. She gave me a slight nod, indicating she thought it would be all right if I told Alfred. After all, Phil knew, so what harm could it do?

I reached into my tote that was under the counter and took out the article. I handed it to Alfred.

Nodding, he said, "I thought that might be the case. You see, Imelda and I have been—*had been*—close friends ever since our spouses died. Imelda's husband was, of course, aware of her family's business, but the two of them never revealed that information to their son.

Imelda thought he'd likely figured it out later on, but he never knew anything about his grandfather's business when he was a child. And her father wanted it that way." He handed back the paper. "Imelda said her father never wanted his grandson to get involved in a life of crime—he regretted having become embroiled in it himself, and he despised the pain it had caused Imelda."

"Does that mean Imelda or her father believed that someone involved in organized crime—a rival perhaps— had been responsible for the death of Randolph Gianetti?" I asked.

"No," he said. "Imelda was positive it was Norah Steele who had vandalized her car. Norah hated Imelda and wanted her out of the picture. When Imelda fled New York, it wasn't for her safety. It was to escape the memories of Randolph. She was devastated by his death and was suffering survivor's guilt. Norah, fearing retribution from Imelda's family, had already gone to ground."

"What do you know about Imelda's husband?" Patty asked. "How did they meet? Did she love him?"

"Did he know about her family before they married?" I asked. "Was he already *in* the family, so to speak?"

He chuckled. "No, he wasn't a member of the crime family. He was a college professor at Brea Ridge Community College. He taught English, and Imelda said he was far removed personality-wise from any other man she'd ever known. Quiet and shy, not boisterous like Randolph or quick-tempered like the men in her family, whose anger and violence was always simmering just beneath the surface."

"She saw her husband as a safe haven then," Patty said.

"Indeed, and she grew to love him very much—maybe even more than she'd loved Randolph."

"Then why had Imelda dug back into Randolph's death?" I asked. "Why had she been searching for evidence that could convict his killer?"

"Because she was afraid," he said. "She'd recently become convinced that there was a target on her back and that it had to do with Randolph's murder. She thought that if she could get Randolph's killer convicted, she and her family would be safe."

I frowned. "Why on earth would Randolph's killer come after Imelda after all these years?"

Flipping his palms, Alfred said, "I have no idea. I tried to convince her she was being irrational. I thought she should talk with a therapist."

"So, you didn't believe the threat was real," Patty said.

"Not until it was too late, no. It caused a lot of tension between us in the days leading up to her death. I'm devastated I didn't take her fears seriously."

Long after both Alfred and Patty left, I sat at my desk with my computer logged onto an auction site and stared unseeingly at the items offered. My mind wasn't on the merchandise. It was on Imelda and Mom and Kurt and secrets from the past.

Chapter Eighteen

Cassie came into the shop, and I wondered if I'd ever looked that young and carefree. Sure, I was just under a decade older than she was, but still. I felt really old today.

"How are you?" Cassie asked.

"I've already had a wild morning." I told her about Patty thinking that our mom might have had a secret baby. "As much as Mom adores rom-coms, if she'd had a secret baby, she'd have already found the baby, introduced us to our older sibling, and possibly reconnected with the father of the baby and planned their wedding by now."

Cassie laughed. "Your family is fun."

I stopped myself before I asked *really* because I remembered that her widowed dad was raising her alone and that he could be somewhat strict much of the time. Maybe *strict* was the wrong word. Gerald was protective, as any good parent would be. But also strict, so....

"Speaking of families, look what I came across yesterday." I showed Cassie the article about the Cappitani family and Randolph Gianetti.

As she scanned the article, I added, "I had that with me at the theater last night. I dropped it, and when Phil picked it up for me, he looked at it and then got angry."

"Why?" she asked.

Shrugging, I said, "I have no idea. But get this. Alfred came by the shop this morning and asked me why Phil got so angry yesterday. He said he'd asked Phil, but Phil wouldn't discuss it with him."

She raised her hand to her mouth. "Did Alfred faint when he saw the article?"

"No. He already knew about Imelda's family's ties to organized crime."

"Wow. Do you think Kurt knows?"

"I have no idea. Can you think of a casual way I could ask?"

Going over to the t-shirt rack, she held up a shirt with *The Godfather* logo. "You could wear this the next time you plan to see him."

I laughed. "That's an idea. Not necessarily a *good* one, but it's an idea."

My phone pinged. I looked down at the screen and saw that I had a text message from Barry. I opened the message to see that he'd sent me a photograph of a young couple. The woman was the same one whose photo Imelda had torn out of the old movie magazine—Norah Steele. The man also looked familiar.

"Look at this." I turned the screen around to Cassie. "Who does this man look like to you?"

"Well, if you age him up about a hundred years, he looks like that old guy who was in here the other day."

"Reggie Flax." I nodded. "I think so too."

I read the message Barry had sent along with the photo: *The woman in this picture is the one that police initially wanted for questioning in the death of Randolph Gianetti. Apparently, she and Randolph were pretty close. I'm guessing she dumped the poor dude in the photo for Gianetti and then maybe wished she hadn't.*

I wrote back: *Well, sit down if you aren't already because that guy—unless I'm sorely mistaken—is Reggie Flax.* I went on to bring him up to speed on Reggie's breaking into Imelda's home and getting arrested.

Barry called. When I answered, he said, "This is too intense for text. Do the police believe Reggie killed Imelda?"

"I don't know," I said, putting him on speaker and alerting him to that fact so that Cassie could participate in the conversation. "Reggie was released on bail for the B&E, and Kurt asked Reggie if he killed Randolph Gianetti. Reggie said no but that he was afraid his wife might have."

"I might have to go pop some corn for the remainder of this call," Barry teased. "Do you believe Reggie is married to Norah Steele?"

"I feel it's a strong possibility. I don't know whether this photo you sent was taken before or after Randolph Gianetti's death; but if it was after, then they apparently either got together or made up after Gianetti was out of the way."

"What are you going to do now?" Cassie asked.

"I'm not sure yet," I said. "I feel obligated to make Kurt and Detective Tilson aware of this new possibility. But first, I'd love to talk with Reggie Flax." After promising to keep Barry updated, I ended the call.

A customer came in, and Cassie left my office, pulling the door up behind her. I heard her greet the customer as I punched in the number Reggie Flax had given us. After two failed attempts to reach him, I left him a message to contact me, and then I called Kurt.

Kurt answered on the first ring. "Dina, hi."

"Hi, there. Have you spoken with Reggie Flax since he was arrested?"

"No. Have you?"

"I haven't. I'm getting ready to text a photo to you. When you get it let me know."

"Got it." He paused, and I supposed he was examining the photo. "Is that Reggie and Norah Steele?"

"I believe it is."

"That explains why Reggie Flax wasn't on the *Usual Suspects* roster," he said.

"True. But do you remember Reggie saying he thought his wife was responsible for murdering Randolph Gianetti? I wonder now if that's truly what he believes or if he merely told us that lie because he killed Gianetti out of jealousy?"

"I have no idea, but I'm going to find out." His voice was grim.

"Good luck. I tried to call Reggie but didn't get an answer. I'm going to call Detective Tilson now and tell her about this new development. She might not feel it's relevant, but she can't say we didn't immediately report our discovery."

"True. And thanks, Dina."

I came close to asking him about the Cappitani family, but I decided this wasn't the right time. Instead, I said I'd talk with him soon and ended the call.

Time to talk with Detective Tilson. But before I could do that, Cassie called out to me. She needed me to answer the customer's question about some *Star Wars* merchandise he was looking for.

It was after lunchtime before I had a chance to reach out to Detective Tilson. When I did, I got her voicemail. I left a message telling her about both the article I'd discovered at the library and the photograph Barry had texted to me. I said that I didn't know if either were relevant but that she had asked Kurt and me to keep her updated.

As I finished the apple I'd brought for lunch, my phone rang. I wrapped the core in a napkin, tossed it into the trash can beside my desk, and answered the call. It was Kurt.

"I spoke with Reggie Flax," he said. His voice was flat, giving no indication of how the conversation had gone.

"And?" I prompted.

"I asked him straight out if his wife was Norah Steele. He told me not to be ridiculous, so I pushed back with the assertion he'd made that he believed his wife might have had something to do with Gianetti's death."

"What did he say to that?" I asked.

"He said he'd been frightened and confused when he'd said that. I asked him what he was looking for inside

Gran's house, and he said he'd been looking for a piece of jewelry—a locket—that he'd given her years ago."

I scoffed. "That makes no sense whatsoever. I'm sure that if she'd had anything that belonged to Reggie, she'd have given it back after he came to visit her at the theater."

"That's what I said. He told me she'd intended to, but then she was killed. His only intention, he vowed, was to reclaim something of pure sentimental value because it had belonged to his mother."

"I'm not buying that."

"I'm not either." He sighed. "But he was evasive and kept talking in circles. When I asked him his wife's name, he finally told me to stop trying to drag Aggie into this— she left me years ago."

Sitting up straighter in my chair, I asked, "Aggie? He said her name was Aggie?"

"Yeah. Why?"

"I wonder if his Aggie is our Agnes?"

Chapter Nineteen

After work, I went to have dinner with Mom and Patty. We were having spaghetti, and I'd stopped by the grocery store to pick up a loaf of garlic bread. If Phil wouldn't give me the answers that I felt I deserved later, I could breathe garlic in his face.

Meanwhile, Patty was interrogating Mom when I walked into the kitchen.

"Please! It can't be that bad!"

"It was bad, and I don't want to discuss it with you." Mom drained the spaghetti. "I wish I'd never said anything about it."

"But you didn't," Patty said. "You merely *hinted* at some deep, dark secret from your past. That's even worse!"

I placed the bread on the counter, hung my tote on a chair, and scooped up Popcorn. "What have I missed?"

"Nothing." Patty huffed and folded her arms.

"Actually, I was talking to Popcorn, but—" I grinned. "Aw, come on, Mom. You know we're going to bug you to death until you tell us what we want to know. You might as well spill the beans over dinner."

"They call it spilling the tea these days." Mom managed to tip her nose into the air as she ladled spaghetti onto three plates. "Put the cat down and go get washed up."

"Yes, ma'am." I gave Patty a mock glare as I walked past her. She'd already got me in trouble with Mom, and I hadn't even been there five minutes yet.

When I came back to the table, Patty was still pouting.

"Mom, Patty is right," I said, as I took my seat. "You always told us that we should feel free to tell you anything. Don't you believe that should be a two-way street?"

"It's in the past. It's not relevant anymore. Just like Imelda's past isn't relevant to Kurt or any of the rest of her family." Mom used her fork to twirl her spaghetti daintily against the bowl of her spoon.

"Is there another baby?" Patty just blurted out the words. "Do Dina and I have a sibling?"

"Oh, for goodness' sake!" Mom's fork clattered against her plate, and she pushed her chair away from the table and left the room.

"Way to go," I hissed.

"You pushed her too," Patty whispered.

"Not like you did. You'd already started when I got here. How long had you been interrogating her?"

"Oh, don't you dare play innocent with me. You want to know Mom's secret every bit as much as I do."

"Maybe so, but I didn't ask her if she had a secret baby." It was hard to whisper yell, but I gave it my best shot.

Mom returned to the table and slapped a photograph down between Patty and me. "There. And hush—you're making Popcorn nervous."

I looked at the photo and then looked at Patty. After sharing a confused glance, we both lowered our eyes to the photograph again.

"Don't you have anything to say?" Mom sat back down and retrieved her spoon and fork. "Now my spaghetti is cold."

"I'll heat it up for you." I stood and reached for her plate, but she waved me away.

"I'm fine. Sit back down and eat."

I did as I was told and threw another guilty gaze in Patty's direction before considering the photo one more time. In it, Mom was standing in a hotel room with a white bed sheet wrapped around her and tied at her left shoulder. Her hair was pulled up in a French twist. "You look lovely, Mom. I'm guessing you went to a toga party?"

Was *that* the horrible secret? Patty and I had done worse things than that. We'd once sneaked out and gone to a college frat party while we were still in high school. We each tasted beer for the first time, thought it was disgusting, and ran all the way back home. Mom and Dad never found out—as far as we knew.

"Not only that." Mom took a deep, steadying breath. "There was a contest. I won Most Virginal Toga."

Patty started making these little snorting noises that cued me into the fact that she was trying not to burst out laughing. Trying to keep it together myself, I didn't dare look at her or Mom. I simply stared down at my plate.

"Well? Where are all the questions?" Mom's voice was stern and serious.

Not trusting myself to say a single syllable, I kept my mouth tightly closed.

With a laugh bubbling up and sneaking into her voice, Patty asked, "Why is that such a bad thing?" She let the giggle spill over just a little bit. "You look really pretty in this picture, and you won a contest—Most *Virginal* Toga. It's not like you won *Trashiest* Toga!"

At that, my own laughter surfaced. Soon, the three of us were wiping tears of laughter from our eyes.

"Seriously, Mom, why didn't you want Patty and me to know this?"

Mom sobered slightly. "That's not all that happened that night."

Patty and I both stiffened.

"There was a young doctor," Mom said. "He was very handsome, and he asked me to take a walk with him. I thought he was enamored of me. He took my hand, and we walked on the beach."

"Sounds romant—" Patty began.

I frowned and shook my head quickly, and she stopped talking. We had no idea what Mom was about to reveal to us.

"Anyway, he led me toward the ocean." She got a dreamy look in her eyes. "We stood there in the warm water, the waves lapping about our thighs, and he gently took my face in his hands and kissed me. He was wearing a toga, too, by the way, and I became aware that he wasn't wearing anything else." Her cheeks flamed.

I clenched my fists. What had this monster done to our mother?

"He…um…well, his kiss became more passionate, and I don't mind telling you the man was a good kisser. But then he began to remove my toga."

Patty gasped.

Mom nodded. "He did. He slipped his hands underneath it and was pulling it up over my hips when he realized I had on my one-piece bathing suit underneath."

"What did you do?" I asked.

"I left him standing in the ocean with that bed sheet slung over his head while I took off like a scalded rabbit."

"Did he come after you?" Patty raised her hand to her mouth.

"Eventually. But by then I was back in my room with the door locked." Mom went back to eating.

"That's the end of the story?" I asked. "I mean, that's not so bad."

"It would have been bad if you'd have found that photograph or saw an article in some newspaper calling me Miss Virginal Toga or something." She sniffed. "The point I was trying to make is that we all have things we don't want aired in public—or at all. As far as any of us know, Kurt has never had anything to do with his great-grandfather's business dealings, and I doubt Imelda did either. That part of her life is none of our business."

"Unless it relates to her death," I said.

"If it does, then you let Detective Tilson chase down that lead. You aren't qualified to deal with a gang of mobsters. Besides, it has never been proven that Imelda wasn't killed by some random person."

"Do you really believe that's what happened to her?" Patty asked.

Mom ate in silence for a moment. "No. But you're my children, and I love you, and I don't want anything bad happening to you. I suffered enough when you were being mistreated by that rotten husband of yours, Patty."

"I know."

That shut us all up, and we ate the rest of the meal in silence. I, for one, was trying the entire time to think of something I could say to lighten the mood, but I couldn't come up with a thing.

Given Mom's admonition at dinner, I didn't rush right over to confront Phil as soon as I saw him. She'd made it clear she didn't want Patty or me poking our nose into Imelda's murder. To be fair, Patty hadn't. I, on the other hand, had made it my mission to learn who'd killed Imelda and why. Did that have anything to do with Imelda's handsome grandson? Maybe. But I'd like to think I wasn't that shallow—that I was seeking justice and trying to get a killer off the streets and protect my sister and the rest of the cast and crew of *Barefoot in the Park*. Helping Kurt was merely a side benefit.

At last, Mom was onstage with Cassie and Billy. I got up from my seat, stretched, and walked around the auditorium. Spotting Phil sitting a few rows back and looking morose, I went and sat down beside him.

"How are you today?" I asked him.

He grunted.

"Listen, I need to talk with you about that article you saw yesterday." I stared hard at him even though he refused to look at me. "What about it made you so angry?"

Phil didn't answer.

"And why don't you like Reggie Flax? Is he somehow associated with this organized crime thing?"

At last, Phil turned and pierced me with a belligerent glare. "I liked Imelda...a lot. When I found out that she and Alfred were only friends, I decided to make a move. She didn't take me seriously at first. I'd known her father in New York, and—" He lowered his eyes.

"Were you sent here to watch over her?"

"Yeah. Her dad paid me to move here. That was a million years ago, though. When the old man died, the checks stopped coming, but it didn't matter. I thought there was no reason to watch over her anymore." He shook his head. "It had been so long ago. I'd watched Imelda from a distance, but eventually we'd both gone on with our lives. She never knew. I was nobody to her until this play. Mr. Cappitani did me a favor getting me out of that life. I've done all right here in Skillet Ridge."

"You never told Imelda you were her bodyguard?" I asked.

He shook his head. "Fine bodyguard I turned out to be, didn't I? Reggie Flax shows up, and the next thing I know, Imelda is dead."

"Wait." I took my phone from my pocket and pulled up the image of Reggie Flax and Norah Steele that Barry had sent me. "I believe this is Reggie. Do you know who this woman is?"

He squinted at my phone. "Yeah, that's Norah."

"Norah Steele, right? She was wanted for questioning in Randolph Gianetti's death, wasn't she?"

"I guess so. What about it?"

"Do you think she did it?"

"Nah, it was that creep, Reggie," he said. "Everybody said it was Norah, but does she look like a dame who knows anything about cars? Reggie knew Gianetti always drove that car around. I knew when he showed up here, there'd be trouble."

"Did you know of an Agnes Harper or Agnes Rollins? I'm thinking Norah Steele might be going by one of those names and that she married Reggie Flax."

Phil scoffed. "Never heard of any Agnes, and no way would Norah have married a jerk like Reggie. If she married anybody, it was for money. I always figured she got out of New York to avoid any retribution over the accident, went to some small town somewhere, and married a rich guy."

"You're probably right," I said.

"I hope you're able to get some evidence to put Reggie Flax in a prison cell for the rest of his life. I knew he was nothing but trouble, and yet, I didn't follow him after he left the theater. Imelda is dead because of me."

"That's not true." I placed my hand on his arm.

He went back to staring at the stage as gray and still as a statue.

"I'm sorry," I said softly, as I got back up and walked away. When I was out of earshot of everyone on stage, I called Kurt and arranged to meet with him at my place after rehearsal.

Chapter Twenty

I was tired by the time I got home, but I was more anxious than ever to find out who killed Imelda and why so we could put the whole matter behind us and begin to get over it. Having all this suspicion hanging over everyone was horrible.

When Kurt arrived, he commented that I looked exhausted. Not what a woman wants to hear from a guy she'd have a romantic interest in if she was sure he wasn't involved in anything shady, but there you go.

"Gee, thanks," I said.

"I didn't mean to be unkind." He gave me a slight smile. "You're still beautiful, but you do look like you'd love nothing more than to go to sleep."

"Thank you." *He said I was beautiful!* I hoped I wasn't blushing. "Be that as it may, I really want us to compare notes and see what we can come up with. You and your family must be desperate to put this matter to rest so you can grieve Imelda properly."

"And you want to make sure your sister and your Mom aren't working with a killer."

"Right." I went into the kitchen and put on a pot of decaffeinated coffee. "Plus, I want to help you get closure. We went through this not so long ago when Patty's estranged husband was murdered. But that's a story for another time. I don't want us to get sidetracked."

A few minutes later, we were seated at the kitchen table with steaming cups of coffee and my laptop between us.

"Where should we start?" Kurt asked.

"Did you ever have any luck contacting Reggie?" At Kurt's headshake, I continued. "We could start there then. I'm not holding my breath, but we might be able to reach him."

Kurt took out his phone, dialed Reggie's number, and the call went to voicemail.

"Could it be that he's afraid to talk with us?" I sipped my coffee. "Or that Detective Tilson told him not to speak with us?"

"That could certainly be the case since she asked us both if we wanted to get a restraining order against him.

Since he's a lost cause for the time being, let's focus on *Aggie*."

I pulled up the social media platform on which I'd originally found Agnes Harper Rollins. Her profile photo was of a poodle, so that didn't help us put a face to a name. Since her account was private, we couldn't see any of her photos.

"Naturally, we have no image of Agnes to compare to Norah Steele."

"But if Agnes *is* Norah, and Gran believed her to have orchestrated the accident that cost Randolph Gianetti his life, then why was Agnes's name on the roster of *Usual Suspects*?" Kurt asked.

"Good point. I suppose it could have been a case of keep your friends close and your enemies closer." I sent her a message and asked her if she was married to Reggie Flax. "Here goes nothing."

Agnes was online, and she immediately responded: *I told you to never contact me again. While my private life is none of your business whatsoever, I'm not married to Reggie.*

Kurt leaned in to read Agnes's message. "That could be a clever out. Reggie told us his wife had left him."

"He did, but he told us so many things that I don't know what to believe anymore." I sent another question: *Were you ever married to Reggie?*

Agnes didn't respond, and the message box showed that she'd logged off the platform.

"Well, that's that." I sighed. "I suppose we could show Mary a photograph of Norah Steele and ask if she'd ever seen that woman at your grandmother's house."

"I don't know." Kurt ran a hand through his hair. "Norah Steele wouldn't look like those magazine photos anymore."

"No, but she might still be recognizable. Wonder if Detective Tilson could do one of those computer-generated aging tricks on one of Norah's magazine pics?"

"I guess." He sounded so dejected.

Placing my hand on his forearm, I said, "We'll find your grandmother's killer."

"You don't know that. I feel like we've been looking for some sort of phantom or something. Every time we get close to a lead, we reach out to catch it, and we end up with a handful of nothing."

I weighed my next words carefully before uttering them. My question could ruin our friendship. But it could also help us in finding Imelda's murderer.

Keeping my eyes on his face but trying not to appear accusatory, I softly asked, "Do you think someone from the Cappitani family—or some rival—could be responsible for your grandmother's death?"

He frowned. "Why would Gran's death have anything to do with my great-grandparents? They've been dead for decades."

"But your grandfather was involved with organized crime…"

Barking out a laugh, he said, "That's ridiculous."

I walked into the living room and took the article about Imelda, her parents, and Randolph Gianetti from my tote. When I returned to the kitchen, Kurt had his arms folded across his chest and was staring at me coldly.

"I'm sorry." I placed the paper in front of him.

He glanced down at it, and then uncrossed his arms to pick up the article and read it carefully. "This is tabloid garbage. I can't believe you took it seriously."

"Do you know Phil from the theater?"

"I met him. Why?" He scoffed. "Is he the godfather or something?"

"No, but he did tell me he was sent here when your grandmother left New York as a sort of undercover protection detail for her."

"Well, he sure did a bang-up job of that, didn't he?" He stood. "Thanks for the coffee. Have a good night."

"Kurt, wait—"

"I need to get home. And you need to keep your nose out of our business."

"I'm sorry—"

My apology fell on deaf ears. The door had already closed behind him.

On Thursday morning, I decided to stop by Mom's house before going to work to check on her, Patty, and Popcorn. Mainly, I wanted to tell Mom she'd been right.

"I should have minded my own business all along," I told her. "My meddling has ruined my friendship with Kurt. He'll probably never speak to me again."

"He will." She patted my shoulder. "He was angry, that's all. And can you blame him? You dropped a bomb on him—one his parents should have told him about years ago."

"And it was organized crime." I looked down to hide my smile. "It wasn't as if I showed him a photo of Imelda winning the Most Virginal Toga contest."

She hit me with her dish towel. "Sit down and I'll make you some breakfast."

"No time. I have a group of seniors coming in this morning for a tour of the shop's exhibits."

"Oh, that'll be nice."

"I hope so. I'm pretty nervous about it."

She rolled her eyes. "You and your sister. Such Nervous Nellies. You'd better eat something. Imagine how embarrassed you'll be if your stomach growls in the middle of your tour."

"Okay. I'll have a slice of toast." I got a piece of bread and put it into the toaster. "I'm guessing Patty is nervous about the play?"

"Yes." Mom got the butter out of the fridge and placed it on the table. "She's afraid she isn't ready. And what if the actors aren't ready? Maybe they should've halted production for a few months out of respect for Imelda. Or at least until after her killer had been brought to justice. What if people think she's heartless to go on with the play? What if no one shows up?"

My toast popped up. I grabbed it out of the toaster and spread butter on it. "That's ridiculous. Where is she now?"

"She's still in bed, and don't you dare wake her. I don't know what time she finally got to sleep. I heard her pacing half the night."

"I'll call her later." I kissed Mom's cheek and took my toast to go.

"You're gonna have crumbs all in your car."

"I'll vacuum it out later. See you after work."

By the time I got to work, I realized that—as usual—Mom was right. If I left my window down the least bit while I was at work, my car would be filled with birds feasting on breadcrumbs when I came out. Good thing I never left my windows down.

I was printing off coupons for the senior group and making sure I had notecards for all my exhibits when Cassie called. She had car trouble this morning, but Billy was on his way to pick her up.

"That's okay." I forced my voice to sound cheerful and positive, like I wasn't on the verge of hysterics.

"We'll be there as soon as possible," she said.

"All righty! The seniors' bus just pulled up outside. I'll see you when you get here. Be careful." I was proud of myself for remembering to throw in that last part. I did want Cassie and Billy to be careful and not rush. But, oh, how I wished they were here already.

"Hi!" I flung open the door, grinning like an idiot. "Welcome to Lights, Camera, Action! I'm so happy you're here."

"We are too, young lady." The man gave me an exaggerated wink.

"I want to see that Conan the Barbarian doll you have," one of the women told me.

"It's actually a mannequin that—"

My voice was drowned out by another woman squealing, "There he is!"

Knowing I needed to get control of the group and actually figuring out how to do that were two different things.

"Coupon!" I shouted above the din.

The group turned en masse. I had their attention.

"I've printed out flyers with twenty percent off coupons for you at the end of the tour." I smiled. "Since Conan has your attention, let's start there." I made my way through the crowd to stand in front of the *Conan the Barbarian* display.

Rifling through my index cards to find my notes on the movie, a movement at the window drew my eye. Reggie Flax had his hands cupped around his face and was looking into the shop. I was torn between motioning him to come inside and finding the card I needed. My first priority was my tour group, so I found the card. When I glanced back up at the window, the man was gone. Had I only imagined he'd been there?

Chapter Twenty-One

Cassie and Billy had arrived midway through the seniors' visit. Once the group left, I sagged against the wall in mock exhaustion.

"Who knew senior citizens could be as wild as a bunch of first graders?" I asked.

"Everybody at the theater," Billy answered with a laugh.

"Thanks for staying, Billy. I'll pay you for your time."

"Nonsense. I took today and tomorrow off from my day job to focus on getting in the proper headspace for the play. I'm getting vacation pay for being here."

"Helping out here certainly doesn't constitute a fun vacation day, so I'll definitely pay you."

Billy gazed at Cassie. "It seems like a pretty great day to me."

Her cheeks pinkened. "We should really get this place tidied up before someone else comes in and thinks the shop has been robbed or something."

"Okay. But when we have the place looking presentable again, I want both of you to take the rest of the day off—with pay—and go do something fun," I said. "Billy's right. You two need to be relaxed and confident before the play tomorrow evening."

It was lunchtime before the shop was neat again and I'd persuaded Billy and Cassie to leave and enjoy the rest of the day. They were good kids, and they deserved to relax. These past few days had been hard on all of us.

The chime over the door sounded, and I turned to see Kurt walking in with a takeout bag. I was surprised. I'd been sure that after asking about his late grandmother's ties to organized crime, I'd destroyed our friendship.

"Hi," I said quietly.

He held up the bag. "I brought apology sandwiches. Hope you haven't had lunch yet."

"I haven't. But I'm the one who should apologize. I should never have—"

"No, you should have. Actually, my parents should have told me years ago about my grandmother's past. We had a long talk last night after I left your place. They didn't know about Phil."

"From the way Phil talked, I don't think Imelda knew either," I said. "He was sent to look out for her from a distance. Her dad didn't want her to know."

"The three of us went to see Phil and invited him to dinner before the play tomorrow evening."

"That's nice." I stepped out from behind the counter. "Would you like to eat in my office?"

"I'd love to." He followed me into the room. "I have turkey and ham."

"I like both, so you choose." I got us each a bottle of water from my mini fridge. "You wouldn't believe the morning I had." Glad I was able to take our conversation into lighter territory, I told him about the seniors' takeover of the shop. "At one point, I even thought I saw Reggie Flax standing outside on the sidewalk with his hands cupped around his face peering inside." I laughed. "Do you think my imagination finally got the best of me?"

Kurt unwrapped the sandwiches and took half of each one, pushing the other two halves across the desk to me. "Who knows? While Reggie *should* have gone home and steered clear of Skillet Ridge until his trial date, it's possible he was desperate enough to find whatever he believed was in Gran's house to stick around. Maybe he was going to ask you to get it for him."

"I don't buy that baloney about the locket." I shook my head. "I can't imagine what he was looking for."

The door chimed, and I hurried to the front.

"Detective Tilson," I said. "Nice to see you." Actually, it was a little unnerving to see her. She hadn't just dropped in to browse the merchandise.

Kurt joined me. "Detective, has something happened?"

"Yes," she said. "I'm glad the two of you are here together. Have either of you seen Reggie Flax today?"

I explained that I thought I'd seen him on the sidewalk this morning while I was entertaining a group of senior citizens but that when I looked again, he was gone.

"What about you, Mr. Marshall? I was told a man matching Mr. Flax's description visited your antique shop this morning and asked to see you but that you weren't in."

"That's right. I had some personal business to attend to and took the morning off."

"You didn't meet up with Mr. Flax elsewhere?" she asked.

"No. What's this about?"

"Reggie Flax allegedly forced his way into your grandmother's neighbor's home this morning and was shot," Detective Tilson said.

"Is he going to be okay?" I asked.

"What neighbor? Mary?" Kurt asked.

Detective Tilson answered Kurt's question first. "Yes, the neighbor was Mary Crumpler." She looked at me. "And, no, Mr. Flax is not going to be okay."

"He's dead?" I raised my hand to my mouth. "But why did he break in on Mary? Is she all right? What happened?"

"The officers who were first on the scene are interrogating Ms. Crumpler at the police station now."

"This is terrible," I said.

Kurt placed a comforting arm around my shoulders. "Has Mr. Flax's wife been notified?"

"Deputies have been sent to his home to inform his wife," Detective Tilson said.

"But he said his wife had left him," I said.

"I'm confident local law enforcement will be able to track her down. I'll be in touch if I need to talk with you again." With a nod, she turned and left.

I was glad Kurt still had his arm around my shoulders. I rested my head against him momentarily.

"This is unbelievable. Poor Reggie." I quickly raised my head to look at Kurt. "I'm so sorry. What I meant to say was—"

"It's all right," he interrupted. "I don't believe Reggie killed Gran either."

"But what was he doing at Mary's house? Could he have wanted something from your grandmother's house so badly that he went to Mary's to ask if she had a key?"

After giving my shoulders one last reassuring squeeze, Kurt dropped his arm and turned to walk back to my office. "That's possible. Remember, Reggie told me he didn't kill Gran but he was afraid his wife might have. If it's true that Reggie's wife is Norah Steele, Reggie might've been convinced that Gran had proof that Norah was responsible for Randolph Gianetti's death and was searching for the evidence so he could destroy it and protect his wife."

I followed him into my office and sat down at my desk. "But why would Mary shoot him?"

"Well, she *did* see him being arrested the other day. She could've thought he'd killed Gran and was coming for her next."

"That tracks. But Detective Tilson didn't say anything about Reggie being armed." I uncapped my water bottle and took a long drink. "And Reggie didn't have a weapon when he broke into your grandmother's house, did he?"

"No, he didn't. If Mary shot an unarmed man—even if he *did* break into her house—she could be in serious trouble with the police." Kurt took a bite from one of the sandwich halves.

"I can't imagine Reggie wouldn't have left immediately when Mary confronted him with that shotgun," I said. "He never struck me as being particularly nervy. In fact, he seemed kinda on the timid side."

"No. I don't see him trying to wrestle the gun away from Mary or charging on ahead while she had the gun trained on him. I believe she was either frightened and reflexively fired the gun or—" He paused. "Or she intended to kill him."

We finished our lunch while discussing the situation.

"Mary seemed to be the type who'd reach for her gun in an instant." I tossed my trash in the wastepaper basket beside my desk. "She'd even named that gun. If I'm not mistaken, she called it Bertha."

"That's right—she did." He shook his head. "And she was awfully proud of it. I just assumed the gun was there to scare people away or to make Mary feel more secure. I didn't dream she'd ever actually use the thing."

"Of course, the next question is, did she intend to only frighten Reggie away, or did she mean to kill him?"

Before Kurt could respond, Patty came into the shop. She hurried into my office before I could even get to the lobby.

"Patty, what's wrong?" I asked.

"I heard about Mr. Flax's death." She dropped onto the chair beside Kurt. "Hi, Kurt."

"Hey, Patty. Dina and I were talking about Reggie before you came in. We were wondering if Mary intentionally killed him or simply wanted to scare him, and the situation got out of hand."

"Who knows, but this is too much. I'm going to cancel the play."

"What? No. You can't." I knelt beside her chair. "You're nervous about the play—I get that. But everything is going to be fine. Better than fine. It's going to be great."

"It is," Kurt agreed. "My parents and I are looking forward to it. It'll be a bright spot in an otherwise horrendous week."

"I don't know." Patty sighed. "Speaking of your grandmother, I have something for you, Kurt. I found it in the dressing room." She rifled through her purse and then took out a folded piece of paper which she then handed to him.

He unfolded the paper, studied it for a few seconds, and then his eyes widened.

"What is it?" I asked.

Wordlessly, he handed me the paper. Imelda had traced a photo of Norah Steele's face. She'd then drawn outside the lines of the tracing to make Norah's face fuller, changed the nose and hairstyle, and added lines to the face.

I slowly raised my eyes to Kurt's. "We have to call Detective Tilson."

Chapter Twenty-Two

W̶hen my call to Detective Tilson went to voicemail, I left her a message that Kurt and I needed to talk with her about Mary.

"Now what?" I asked.

"Call the police station and ask for her there," Patty said. "This is too important to let go."

"You're right. She needs to know that we suspect Mary of being Nora Steele before Mary is released from jail." I looked up the police station's website and called the number listed. After waiting for what seemed like an eternity, an officer came on the line. "I'd like to speak with Detective Tilson please. My name is Dina Merrill, and I believe I have pertinent information about one of her ongoing cases."

"Of course. Let me connect you to her direct—"

"I tried that," I interrupted. "My call went straight to voicemail. I was hoping maybe she was there at the station."

"No. I'm afraid she's out at the moment."

"I'm calling about Mary—?" I looked at Kurt.

"Crumpler," he supplied.

"Mary Crumpler," I said. "She was brought in after shooting a man who came into her house earlier today."

"Yes?" the officer prompted.

"I…um…is she still in custody?"

"Let's see…. Mary Margaret Crumpler has been released on her own recognizance."

"Thank you." I ended the call and looked at Kurt. "How sure are we that Mary Crumpler is Norah Steele?"

"I can't speak for you but based on my grandmother's enhancements to this photograph combined with her murdering Reggie, I'm positive."

"When Reggie was talking to you about his wife, is it possible he said *Maggie* rather than *Aggie*?" I asked.

"It's possible I misheard him." He frowned. "Mary Margaret—Maggie."

"Whose stage name was Norah Steele. We need to get to Mary's house and confront her." I took a deep breath.

"Let's hope they took her gun into evidence and didn't give it back."

"You stay here," he said. "I'll go. You've done more than enough already."

"I'm not going to let you go confront that woman alone. If what we believe is true, then she's a sociopath who won't hesitate to kill you too." I stood, wiped my damp palms down the sides of my jeans, and grabbed my purse. "I'll lock up the shop and go with you."

"I can stay here and look after the shop until you get back," Patty said.

"Hopefully, we won't be long," I told her.

"All I ask is that you be careful and do not underestimate this woman. She might be old, but from the sound of things, she's extremely dangerous."

"I'll be fine." I gave her a quick hug.

Kurt extended his arm. "Lead the way."

Kurt and I had planned our strategy on our way over to Mary's house; but now that we were almost there, I could feel my nerves gathering into a tight knot in my stomach.

We could be wrong. How could Imelda have lived next door to Mary for so long without realizing who she was? Of course, people didn't socialize with their neighbors the way they once did, but still....

Gayle Leeson

Putting the car into park in Mary's driveway, Kurt looked at me. "Ready?"

I nodded. "I'm glad we're doing this together."

"Yeah, at least, one of us might live to tell the story."

My eyes widened.

Kurt laughed. "It was my silly attempt at dark humor to lighten the mood."

"Um…yeah. I'll say it was dark." I gave him a rueful smile. "Let's go."

We got out of the car and went to Mary's door. Skippy started barking on the other side of the door as soon as I knocked.

"Get back, sweetie, and let's see who it is," I heard Mary say.

I had no doubt she knew exactly who was there.

She opened the door, and I plastered a smile onto my face.

"Hi!" I said. "We heard you had some trouble this morning, and we wanted to come and make sure you're okay."

"Yes," Kurt chimed in. "Is everything all right?"

"Everything is fine. Well, everything except that unfortunate man who broke into my house. He's not fine." She made no move to allow us into the house.

"I'm sure you're in shock." I stepped closer to the door.

"I imagine that's far enough, dear," she said.

Frowning, I asked, "What are you talking about? You aren't going to invite us in?"

She barked out a harsh laugh. "I see why you own a movie memorabilia shop and aren't acting in movies yourself." She jerked her chin toward Kurt. "How about you? What caliber of performance are you capable of?"

"Mary, I don't know what you're talking about," he said. "We heard that Reggie Flax tried to break in on you, so Dina asked her sister to watch the shop so we could come make sure you're okay."

"Reggie *did* break in on me. That is undisputed."

Our plan was already unraveling. We'd expected Mary to invite us in, but it was apparent she had no intention of doing so.

I tried to say something provocative to turn the conversation the way we hoped it would go. "And Bertha did her job."

Grinning, Mary said, "She did."

"I imagine you're frightened now that the police have your gun." I knew she had no reason to be frightened, but it was worth a try.

"You don't believe Bertha was my only security guard, do you?" Her eyes glinted.

"Is that why we can't see your hands?" Kurt asked. "Is one of your security guards pointed at us right now?"

Mary nodded.

"But why?" I asked. "Do you think Kurt and I are in cahoots with Reggie or something? That we're thieves?"

"Once again, dear, I don't think you're going to ever win an Oscar. The best thing you can do is get off my stoop, get into your car, and drive away."

"I'm not going to do that." Kurt's voice was calm.

I whirled my head around to look at him. Was he crazy? This was absolutely not in the plan.

"You don't think I'll shoot you?" she asked.

He shrugged. "If you killed my grandmother and Reggie, you might as well. What's one more? I just ask that you let Dina leave."

"Don't forget Randolph," I said quietly, my voice no way near as steady as Kurt's. I turned back to look at Mary. "If you're Norah Steele, then you killed him too."

"That was an accident!" She screwed up her face as if she were in pain. "I loved Ran. He was *mine*. It was supposed to be *her* in that car. Imelda Cappitani ruined my life!"

"By allowing her fiancé to drive her car?" I asked.

"By taking him from me in the first place." She raised the rifle she'd had hidden by the doorframe to her shoulder. "And you're both right. I've killed three people now—the love of my life, my worst enemy, and my worthless husband. I might as well do away with the two of you as well."

"Not so fast." I put my hands on my hips. "You've gotten away with all of it so far. You won't if you kill Kurt and me."

"I won't if I *don't* kill the two of you."

"You stand an excellent chance," I said. "What proof do we have? A photo of Norah Steele that Imelda filled in to make it resemble you? I've seen enough makeup tutorials online to know that with a little shading and artistic talent, some people can make anyone look like anything. That's pretty flimsy evidence in any court of law."

"She's right," Kurt added. "Who's going to believe that a little old lady carried out a vendetta that spanned— what? Half a century?"

Mary shrugged but made no move to lower the gun.

"Why did you kill Reggie?" I asked.

"He threatened to turn me in—just like the two of you are doing. In fact, he told me he came to see you both to see if one of you would come here with him to talk with me." She sneered. "Had either of you been where you belonged, Reggie might still be alive. Think about *that*."

"How did the two of you even end up together?" I frowned. "Did you fall for him after Randolph died?"

"No, I didn't fall for him." She scoffed. "I needed to get out of New York, and he had the money to help me. Or, rather, his family did."

"Why did you kill Gran?" Kurt asked. "You'd made a new life for yourself. Why wasn't that enough? And if you'd moved here with the intention of murdering her, why did you wait for so long?"

"It took ages to find her here in this little nothing of a town. She absolutely ruined my life. Don't you get that?" She glared at us. "Had I married Ran, I'd have been a star. We'd have traveled the world together—done so much...*had* so much. But, no, the wrong person died, and I became a nobody."

"Talk about putting all your eggs in one basket." Kurt huffed. "My grandmother's life didn't turn out the way she initially hoped it would either, but she made the best of it and went on to have a wonderful home here, a devoted husband she loved, and a son she adored. She was proof that one incident doesn't have to derail your entire life."

"One incident destroyed my life." Mary squinted down the barrel of the gun.

It was your own fault. I wisely didn't voice that thought aloud.

Kurt and I ducked to the left and right of the door, respectively, out of the line of fire. Mary would have to come out the door to shoot us now. If she did come out onto the stoop, maybe one of us—I was hoping Kurt— would be able to rush her and wrestle the rifle away from her.

In unison, he and I turned at the sound of a car barreling up the driveway. It was Detective Tilson. She put the car in park, turned off the engine, and stayed behind the open driver's side door for cover. Raising her service weapon, she called for Mary to lower her weapon.

"Toss the rifle onto the ground in front of the porch and slowly come out with your hands up," Detective Tilson instructed.

"I will, but these two were harassing me! Thank goodness you're here!" Mary opened the door and gingerly lobbed the rifle onto the grass. "I was so scared. They were accusing me of such horrible things." She stepped out onto the stoop with her hands raised.

"You're never gonna win an Oscar either," I muttered.

Detective Tilson closed the car door, reached around with her left hand, and retrieved her handcuffs. "I have no idea what they might've been accusing you of, but I found an outstanding warrant against you in the state of New Jersey." She walked over, brought Mary's arms down, and snapped the handcuffs onto her wrists. "I'm also aware that you were married to Reggie Flax, and I'm arresting you on suspicion of murder."

As she led Mary to her car, she stopped reciting Mary's rights long enough to tell Kurt and me that she'd be talking with us later. We found out from Patty when we returned to Lights, Camera, Action! that Detective Tilson had come in there looking for me to follow up on my phone call when she was alerted that Mary Crumpler had an arrest warrant outstanding in New Jersey.

"When I told her that's where you and Kurt were, she raced out of here as if your lives depended on her," Patty said.

"They very well might have." I hugged Patty. "Thank you for staying here and potentially saving Kurt and me. Let's just not mention this to Mom, okay?"

Epilogue

*B*arefoot in the Park was a success. I even video called Barry so he could watch with me virtually from the front row. After all, he'd been a crucial help in discovering who'd killed Imelda and why.

Kurt and his parents were appreciative of Patty's moving dedication to Imelda, given before the curtain went up, and I saw his mom dabbing tears from her eyes. And yet, she did laugh at the antics of the character which was supposed to have been performed by Imelda and was now accomplished by Mom.

Mom did a wonderful job with her role. I'm afraid that now that the acting bug has bitten her, Patty will never be able to do a play without Mom wanting a role in it again. But that's okay—as long as they both enjoy it.

After the play, Kurt donated Imelda's signed Robert Redford photograph to be displayed in the lobby of the theater. Cassie's dad made a nice case for it, and Patty had a small gold plaque engraved with the words, *In Loving Memory of Imelda Marshall.*

While we were standing in the lobby admiring the tribute, I asked Kurt what he'd found in Imelda's safe deposit box.

"Only her engagement ring from Randolph Gianetti." He gave me a sad smile. "It's beautiful. I gave it to Mom to hold onto for me. Who knows? It might come in handy one of these days."

"I believe Imelda would like that."

"So do I," he said.

Have you read the prequel, *Terminated: He Won't Be Back*? If not, visit Gayle online to find out where to get the free book:

https://www.gayleleeson.com/

Test Your Movie Trivia Knowledge

1. Who directed the film *Casablanca*?

A) Michael Curtiz

B) Sidney Lumet

C) Randolph Gianetti

D) John Ford

2. In what year was *Casablanca* released?

A) 1964

B) 1933

C) 1942

D) 1975

3. Who played the lead role of Rick Blaine in the movie?

A) Gary Cooper

B) Humphrey Bogart

C) Clark Gable

D) Clint Eastwood

4. What was the name of the character played by Ingrid Bergman?

A) Ilsa Lund

B) Maxine Englebright

C) Amanda Tucker

D) Amy Flowers

5. What is the famous line often misquoted as "Play it again, Sam"?

A) "What was the name of that song? Play it, Sam."

B) "That song you played for her. Play it for me."

C) "Play 'As Time Goes By' or you're fired, Sam."

D) "Play it, Sam. Play 'As Time Goes By.'"

6. Which city serves as the setting for most of the film?

A) Paris, France

B) Casablanca, Morocco

C) Berlin, Germany

D) London, England

7. What is the name of the nightclub owned by Rick in the movie?

A) Sam's Piano Bar

B) Rick's Place

C) Rick's Café Américain

D) Cherchez La Femme

8. Who is Rick's loyal friend and piano player at the nightclub?

A) Louis (played by Sam Donaldson)

B) Max (played by Gary Cooper)

C) Bob (played by Bobcat Goldthwait)

D) Sam (played by Dooley Wilson)

9. Which actor portrayed the corrupt police captain Louis Renault?

A) Claude Rains

B) Paul Henreid

C) Leslie Howard

D) Cary Grant

10. Which song is prominently featured in the film and is often associated with *Casablanca*?

A) "La Marseillaise"

B) "As Time Goes By"

C) "All I Ask of You"

D) "Hopelessly Devoted to You"

Answer Key:

1) A

2) C

3) B

4) A

5) D

6) B

7) C

8) D

9) A

10) B

Also by Gayle Leeson

Down South Café Mystery Series

The Calamity Café

Silence of the Jams

Honey-Baked Homicide

Apples and Alibis

Fruit Baskets and Holiday Caskets

Truffles and Tragedy

Pickled to Death (Novella)

Ghostly Fashionista Mystery Series

Designs on Murder

Perils and Lace

Christmas Cloches and Corpses

Buttons and Blows

Have Yourself a Scary Little Christmas (Novella)

Secrets and Sequins

Literatia Series (Portal Fantasy Mystery Series written as G. Leeson)

Saving Piglet (Prequel)
An Eyre of Mystery
A Tale of Two Enemies

Kinsey Falls Chick-Lit Series

Hightail It to Kinsey Falls
Putting Down Roots in Kinsey Falls
Sleighing It in Kinsey Falls

Victoria Square Series (With Lorraine Bartlett)

Yule Be Dead
Murder Ink
Murderous Misconception
Dead Man's Hand
Tea For You (Recipe Ebook)

Embroidery Mystery Series (Written as Amanda Lee)

The Quick and The Thread
Stitch Me Deadly
Thread Reckoning

The Long Stitch Goodnight
Thread on Arrival
Cross-Stitch Before Dying
Thread End
Wicked Stitch
The Stitching Hour
Better Off Thread

Cake Decorating Mystery Series (Written as Gayle Trent)

Murder Takes the Cake
Dead Pan
Killer Sweet Tooth
Battered to Death
Killer Wedding Cake

Myrtle Crumb Mystery Series (Written as Gayle Trent)

The Party Line (short story/prequel)
Between A Clutch and a Hard Place
When Good Bras Go Bad
Claus of Death
Soup…Er…Myrtle!
Perp and Circumstance

ABOUT THE AUTHOR

Gayle Leeson is a *USA Today* bestselling, award-winning author known for infusing her stories with humor and heart. She and her family live in SW Virginia and North Carolina.

If you enjoyed this book, Gayle would appreciate your leaving a review. If you don't know what to say, there is a handy book review guide at her site (https://www.gayleleeson.com/book-review-form). Gayle invites you to sign up for her newsletter and receive excerpts of some of her books:
https://forms.aweber.com/form/14/1780369214.htm

Social Media Links:
Twitter:

https://twitter.com/GayleTrent

Facebook:

https://www.facebook.com/GayleLeeson/

BookBub:

https://www.bookbub.com/profile/gayle-leeson

Goodreads:

https://www.goodreads.com/author/show/426208.Gayle_
Trent

Have You Met Gia?

Excerpt from *An Eyre of Mystery*

Chapter One

*W*ere am I? These buildings...the streets—
nothing looks normal. Nothing looks
modern. And the smell. Ugh. It nearly made
me gag. I looked down and saw I was
standing beside a pile of fresh horse dung. The horse
swished its tail as it passed.

"—goa raight to t' divil then!"

"Huh?" At the sound of the brusque female voice, I
raised my chin. "Are you talking to me?"

She was. Or, rather, she had been. Now the forbidding
old woman dressed like she'd just stepped out of a Brontë
novel shook her head, put her nose in the air, and strode
on. What was that she'd said? Was it even English?

Realizing my own clothes felt a bit strange, I glanced
down at the fancy, floor-length skirt I was wearing. It was

a dark red satin with white and gray stripes. I imagined the bonnet tied at my throat matched it.

Am I in costume? Maybe I was in a play. No. There wouldn't be real horse dung in a play. Besides, I wasn't on a stage.

Either way, I needed to get my butt out of the middle of the road.

My mind raced as I hurried to the sidewalk. What's the last thing I remember? *I was in the library and saw that odd glowing letter L on the cover of Jane Eyre. I touched it and—*

"Now then. Come along."

It was Mr. Briggs. I knew him. I mean, I didn't know him and didn't know how I knew him, but...but I did. He was Mr. Briggs, the attorney from Jane Eyre. He led me down the macadamized street.

"Wh-what are we doing?" I asked.

"He's asked for you, and you indicated you wanted to see him." He frowned down at me. "Have you changed your mind?"

"No." I reached out and took Briggs' arm—I needed the support, but I also craved proof he was real. He was. As real as anything in this place. Had I fallen? Hit my head? Was this a dream? If so, it was the most vivid I'd ever experienced.

Briggs escorted me into a prison and spoke briefly with a jailer, who then led us to a cell. I was behind Briggs, so I couldn't see inside the cell at first.

The jailer pinched my shoulder.

I yelped in surprise and glared at him. "What was that for?"

"You don't belong here." His voice was a menacing hiss; and when he bared his teeth at me, a silverfish darted through them.

The tingling started at my scalp and worked its way through my spine. Still, I managed to lift my head slightly. I inherently knew I couldn't show this creature any hint of fear.

Briggs moved aside, and I turned away from the jailer and stepped closer to the bars.

"Edward," I whispered. Edward Rochester, the brooding hero of Jane Eyre.

"Jane. Darling, Jane." He reached for my hands through the bars.

I put my hands out, and he squeezed them.

Staring into my eyes, he said, "Wait. You aren't— He addressed Mr. Briggs then. "May we have a bit of privacy?"

"Of course. I'll be in the other room with the jailer." Mr. Briggs patted my forearm before walking away.

"Who are you?" Edward asked quietly.

"I'm Gia."

"Did Cooper send you?"

Cooper—the man who'd hired me as archivist for the Smithmore Manor library this morning.

"Yes," I said. Maybe Cooper had sent me, and maybe he hadn't, but yes seemed to be the safest answer under the circumstances.

Edward blew out a breath of relief. It wasn't pleasant. Didn't they have toothpaste in the 1840s? Gum? Mints? I'd have to look into that.

"What are you doing in prison?" I asked.

"I'm to be hanged in five days for the murder of my wife."

"Murder? No one killed Bertha. She committed suicide after setting the fire."

He shook his head. "There was no fire, and Bertha was murdered."

"You—?"

"No," he interrupted. "Not me. You need to find out who did kill her and work with Briggs to get me exonerated. I'm from your world; but if I die in this world, I'm dead in both." He paused. "Same goes for you."

I gulped. "That's good to know."

It wasn't, Reader. It wasn't good to know in the slightest.

"We have few allies here and many enemies."

"Oh, I've already made an enemy," I said. "The jailer pinched me! Then he told me I didn't belong here. And when I looked up at him, there was a silverfish in his mouth. Do you people not have toothpaste?"

"He is a silverfish. They destroy books. You're here to preserve the book—and, hopefully, my life."

"Okay, how do I—?"

"Time to go, Miss Eyre." Briggs had returned.

"Please," I said, "can't we have a few minutes more? I have so many questions."

"The jailer won't permit it. Perhaps we may return in a day or two."

"A day or two? We only have five!"

Edward pressed my hands before letting them go. "Cooper must have faith in you, so I do as well. Go and use the utmost caution."

I nodded. *What have I gotten myself into?*

Briggs helped me into a hansom cab and instructed the driver to take me to Thornfield Hall.

Thornfield Hall—the Rochester home. I tried to swallow the lump that had formed in my throat. *Wonder what awaits me there?*

"I have things to attend to in town, my dear, but I'll be around to check on you later this afternoon," he told me.

There weren't any silverfish in his mouth, as far as I could tell. I thanked him and was relieved for some time alone.

Taking a closer look at my outfit, I had to admit that the person who'd fashioned it had done an excellent job. It certainly felt authentic. The reticule hanging from my left wrist was gray with a floral bouquet embroidered on the front and tassels at the corners. I'd noticed the purse earlier but now took the opportunity to see what was inside—hopefully, a piece of hard candy for my uncomfortably dry mouth.

I untied the drawstring and pulled the fabric apart. Inside was a small fan, some coins, a lace-edged handkerchief, and a folded piece of tan paper. Snatching the paper out of the purse, I opened it and read:

Gia, if you're reading this, you've taken your first journey into Literatia. Congratulations! No, you aren't crazy; you aren't dreaming; you aren't comatose; you aren't dead; you aren't whatever else you might believe you are. You're actually in another world—a book world—and you must recalibrate that world before the silverfish entirely destroy the book. But no worries. I have the utmost faith in your abilities. Fond regards, Cooper Wellingham

Staring down at my employer's words, I said aloud, "This has to be a dream."

The words on the note immediately disappeared and were replaced with: *It isn't. I already told you that.*

"Wait. I can talk with you using this paper?"

Again, like some sort of weird voice-to-text device that worked in reverse or backward or upside down or something, the paper was erased, and new words appeared.

In a way. I told you when you accepted the job this morning that you were taking on a challenging role. You indicated you enjoyed challenges.

"Well, yeah, but not sci-fi, world-hopping challenges that include people with silverfish in their teeth. This is way too out of the box for me."

Had I believed you were not up to the task, I'd have never allowed you to embark upon this journey. If you aren't receptive, I need to pull you out and get someone inside who is willing to help Mr. Rochester immediately.

"I never said I wasn't willing to help Mr. Rochester." I huffed. "Of course, I am. I just—" I chewed on my lower lip for a second. "Get in here and help me already."

Unfortunately, I cannot. I'd be recognized immediately in Literatia, and the silverfish would work quickly to devour the book and everything in it. That includes Mr. Rochester and you in case you hadn't guessed.

"Mr. Rochester told me that if we die in the book, we die. Period. Am I getting hazardous duty pay for this gig? Because we never talked about my risk of dying. I figured my biggest threat would be a papercut."

Finish your task successfully, and you will be rewarded.

I wasn't making myself clear. I needed to reframe my question and stop being flippant. "What are the odds of my dying here?"

The words previously written faded out, but new words didn't come right away.

"Did you hear me?" I asked.

Low. Under all but the most extreme circumstances, I will be able to extricate you before you die.

"Oh." I slumped against my seat in relief. "And you can get Rochester out too, right?"

No. His life is in your hands.

"But he's your guy. He knew you sent me before I knew you sent me. You can't just leave him in there. In fact, why can't you take us both out of here now?"

I'm unable to remove Rochester. If I get you out, Rochester will die, and the literary classic Jane Eyre will never have existed. That has farther-reaching ramifications in our world and in Literatia than you realize. I will ask you once again, are you up to this challenge?

"I am."

Good.

"I'll keep this paper with me at all times so that I can communicate with you as necessary."

This is the only communication we can have until you return. If you were to be found with this paper, you'd be hanged as a witch.

"The last witch hanging in England took place in the late 1600s."

Trust me, they'll make an exception. Now, I'll leave you with a few words of clarification: Not everyone is who they seem or have the same personalities as those they originally embodied in the book. One of those characters killed Rochester's wife. Bring that person to justice, free Rochester, and you will be brought home. Godspeed.

Starting at one corner, the paper turned to ash. I realized Cooper was burning it on the other side. I brushed it onto the floor of the cab and watched it completely turn to dust.

This morning I'd started what I guessed would be a boring but nice job as an archivist at a gorgeous manor house in the hills of North Carolina. Now it wasn't even lunchtime, and I was responsible for a man's life, trying to avoid being killed myself, and tasked with keeping Jane Eyre safe for readers everywhere.

The cab came to a stop. I took out a coin and pulled the drawstring to close my reticule when I heard the driver climbing down from his seat.

"I thought I heard you talking," he said, upon opening the door and helping me out. "Me wife was a praying woman too."

I smiled. "Too bad she isn't here. I could use all the help I can get."

Interested in reading more? Visit Gayle online at www.gayleleeson.com for more information.